James N. Matthews

My Holiday

How I Spent It - Being Some Rough Notes of a Trip to Europe and Back, in the

Summer of 1866

James N. Matthews

My Holiday

How I Spent It - Being Some Rough Notes of a Trip to Europe and Back, in the Summer of 1866

ISBN/EAN: 9783337144883

Printed in Europe, USA, Canada, Australia, Japan

Cover: Foto ©Andreas Hilbeck / pixelio.de

More available books at **www.hansebooks.com**

MY HOLIDAY;

HOW I SPENT IT:

*BEING SOME ROUGH NOTES OF A TRIP
TO EUROPE AND BACK,*

IN THE SUMMER OF 1866.

BY

JAMES N. MATTHEWS.

BUFFALO:
MARTIN TAYLOR, PUBLISHER.
NEW YORK:
HURD & HOUGHTON.
1867.

PRINTED BY MATTHEWS & WARREN,
BUFFALO, N. Y.

TO

JULIUS MOVIUS, Esq.,

A friend of many days,

THIS LITTLE BOOK IS RESPECTFULLY DEDICATED, AS A
MARK OF THE AFFECTIONATE REGARD
IN WHICH HE IS HELD BY

THE AUTHOR.

PREFACE.

The greater portion of the following pages were printed as " *Editorial Correspondence* " in a daily newspaper, the BUFFALO COMMERCIAL ADVERTISER. The considerations that led to their publication originally are set down at the beginning of the first letter. When it is added that similar reasons have induced the writer to gather them up, correct, add to, and put them out in this shape, critics will learn (should the poor little book, indeed, fall into the hands of any such august personages) that no attempt to cheat the great reading public is intended, and all is said, then, that need be said in the way of preface.

M.

CONTENTS.

IV.

V.

VI.

VII.

VIII.

IX.

X.

XI.

scenes and sights, that they have become a drug in
the editorial market; and as I was not going to tread
any unfrequented paths, I could not hope to vary
their monotony. I stated these objections so plainly
that I am sure you have not expected to hear from
me, except in brief private notes, and I can readily
imagine that you will experience a sensation — of as-
tonishment certainly, and of pleasure I hope — when
you recognize the cross, crabbed hand of your venerable *collaborateur* in such a lengthy epistle as this is
likely to turn out. But if you attribute this compli-
ance with your request to any unselfish motives, you
will be mistaken, and I must hasten to undeceive you,
lest you should give me more credit than I deserve.
Know then that the chief inducement which prompts
me to write this letter, and which will prompt me to
write others if others should follow this, is to save
myself trouble. Strange as this assertion may sound,
it is easily explained. I have now been in Europe a
week, and it is time that I should write some letters
to private friends, if not to readers of the *Commercial*. I cannot write to all who asked me to do so,
nor even to those whom I would most desire to
please; but it has occurred to me that by availing
myself of your columns I could make one letter do
the work of many, as it would most likely be seen
there by all who expressed a desire to hear from me.
Hence this result.

This explanation begets another. As my letters

will have for their main object the gratification of private friends, the general reader will not, I fear, discover much of interest in them; for I frankly confess that to make readable letters is only a secondary consideration with me. I must, therefore, make use of my interest with you, and stipulate that when you publish a letter of mine you shall give it as " extra matter," and not curtail your usual variety to make room for it. I shall then feel justified in requesting all who feel no interest in my epistles to pass them by, and to remember that if they are worth nothing they cost nothing also, and so no one will be cheated. If this fact is kept in remembrance I shall write under less restraint: and with this much of explanation I can pass on to my task.

I left New York on Saturday, the twenty-sixth day of May, in the steamer *Bremen*, of the North German Lloyd line, Captain H. A. F. Neynaber, bound for Bremen, with two hundred and thirty-three passengers and a trifle over a million of dollars in specie. There was but one person on the ship whom I had ever seen before, and he, a friend from Albany, was in the same state-room with me. I suppose most persons have realized what it is to bid good-bye to one's home, but those who have not been about to put the great sea between them and home, can hardly appreciate the choking emotions which crowd upon the passenger for Europe as the ship leaves her dock. It is an interesting sight. The wharf is crowded with friends who come to bid "God-speed" to the voyagers, weeping, shouting and waving handkerchiefs. The passengers — almost to a woman as well as man — try to keep up a brave appearance, but the smiles are frequently mingled with queer contortions of the countenance. A gun is fired, a band strikes up, a great shout is given, and the ship glides out of the dock. Everybody on shore rushes toward the end of the wharf, everybody on the ship crowds to where they can see their friends — shore and ship are alive with waving handkerchiefs, and, in less than two minutes it seems, distance renders recognition impossible. The excitement on the ship dies out very suddenly, the passengers gather into small and melancholy groups, and I fear that but few of them really enjoy the sail down the magnificent harbor and bay of New York. I suppose this is the regular scene as every steamer leaves port. I know that the passengers of the *Bremen* were a sad-looking set of beings, and I admit that your humble servant, albeit a man not much given to the melting mood, discovered a mist coming between his vision and the objects he was looking at. The day was a lovely one, and I think an *excursion* down to the mouth of the Hudson must be very enjoyable, but the Europe-bound traveler is too busy with sad thoughts to realize the beauties of the scene.

It is not my intention to detail my experiences on the voyage, though, more for the sake of having something to do than for any other reason, I noted all I could observe every day. On looking over this diary now, however, I discover but little that would interest even those who feel most interest in the writer. Perhaps the Notes may be useful hereafter, when I wish to beguile away a dull hour by taking the trip over again, in imagination. At any rate I hope so — else there is much labor lost. There are the usual comments upon the incidents of the day — the usual speculations upon fellow passengers, some of which afterward proved to be curiously correct and others quite as curiously incorrect — the usual record of the ship's progress, the most interesting fact of each day's history — the usual description of the first sunset at sea — and, in short, the usual humdrum record of a prosperous voyage across the Atlantic. There was not even a fit of sea-sickness to describe, which was something of a disappointment, for I had flattered myself that my description would make somebody as sick as I was. Nor had I, therefore, an opportunity to try many of the various remedies which were recommended by kind and experienced friends. True, I did feel a few qualms about the stomach the first day at dinner time, and I tried an experiment with a sailor's belt, which I had bought upon the injunction of a friend who knew it to be infallible. I put it on; every time I felt a qualm I tightened the belt, as I was instructed to do; and I was not seasick: *but,* as I took some champagne at the same time (another remedy), and had finally to take off the belt or breathe my last breath, it is hard to decide which preventive is entitled to my recommendation. I know I tried them both faithfully, but found I could stand another glass of champagne better than another reef in the belt. I was quite gratified, however, to discover that I had a waist once more, though it would not bear as much squeezing as I could wish.

This brings me to the conclusion that a man must draw upon his imagination for his facts, if he expects to make up an interesting record of incidents on a passage to Europe in a steamship ; and my imagination, you know, would not respond to many drafts, even of a small denomination. It must suffice to say that we had a remarkably pleasant and quick trip (within four hours of the quickest ever made between New York and Bremen) — that the ship touched at Cowes (near Southampton) at three o'clock on Wednesday morning, a little more than ten days out — that I was gratified and surprised there by a visit at that early hour from a Buffalo friend, who had heard of my coming — that after landing our passengers for England, and the specie (the latter in a very unceremonious way as it seemed to me), we proceeded on our voyage and reached Bremerhaven at four o'clock, the seventh of June, having made the passage in less than twelve days, counting the difference in time, from New York. I will spare your readers all my memoranda of feelings at first sight of land, of the beauties of the Isle of Wight and the white cliffs of Dover, and the reluctance with which I passed my native island, without stopping, after twenty years of absence; nor will I detail the proceedings of the passengers just before we landed, further than to say that they were very complimentary and gratifying to the Captain; but I will get ashore as quick as possible.

Bremerhaven is thirty miles below Bremen, and is the harbor at which vessels of large burthen have to stop, though their nominal destination is the latter port. A train was in waiting for us, and we were deposited in an elegant railway station at Bremen after a ride of about an hour and a-half, through a very flat, poor and uninteresting country. Bremen being a free city, there was no examination of our baggage, which was transferred to the *Hotel de l'Europe*, a fine house, without trouble and at very little expense. A sound night's sleep in a good big bed was an incident worth recording, after nearly two weeks of semi-suffocation in the narrow berth of a steamer.

Very little is said in the Guide Books about Bremen, yet I would advise every one who goes to Europe by way of that port to stop there a day or two at least. They will find much to interest them. As I had to leave before noon of next day, I got up very early, and in company with a lady who had been placed in my charge as soon as the ship touched port (as she was coming direct to Dresden), I drove about the city for two hours. It is a quaint old town of nearly seventy-five thousand inhabitants, and has many curious and some very fine buildings. The most interesting to my eye is the *Rathhaus*, or town hall, which is more than four and a half centuries old, and one of the finest specimens of the florid gothic style of architecture I have ever seen. We visited the famous cellars beneath this building, where we saw enormous casks, covered with elaborate carvings, and filled with costly wines. In one was hock, said to be more than one hundred and fifty years old. I longed for a taste of it, but the price per glass — something over three dollars — was more than I had purse for; so we contented ourselves with drinking "the memory of Washington" in some delicious hock made in the year that the first American Congress met. The *Dom* (Lutheran Cathedral) was originally a Romanesque building, built in the year 1160. Additions having been made to it at different times, in various styles of architecture, its aspect now is very curious and venerable. Another fine church (St. Ausgarius) has a spire three hundred and twenty-five feet high. We saw a stone statue of a man eighteen feet high, so old that its history is almost a myth. It is called a *Rolandsäule*, and is supposed to be a symbol of the rights and privileges of the town. We saw many other objects worth noting, but inexorable haste forbade our obtaining any reliable particulars about them. The pleasantest feature of the town, to us, was the exquisite taste manifested in decorating the dwellings with beautiful flowers. With the rich this is done to an extraordinary degree. Most of the large houses have glass balconies in front filled with flowers, and many of the occupants were taking breakfast almost in the open air, as it were. But all the poor houses, also, manage to make a pretty show of vines and bushes, and almost all have a little arbor in the Lilliputian garden, into which the honest family contrive to squeeze themselves for an out-door meal.

But I must not linger longer in Bremen, or I shall never get to Dresden, or to the end of this letter. It is necessary to go to the railway station at least an hour before the train starts, for though you can get into Bremen without trouble, you cannot go further into the interior until your baggage has been examined. Here my troubles commenced. I had been entrusted by a friend with a valuable revolver and a pretty heavy package of cartridges to deliver to a relative of his in Dresden. These I had with great care wedged into my largest trunk, so that they would not move about and spoil other articles. By the help of a German friend another trunk and satchel had passed the scrutiny without trouble, and I was, with a good deal of vigorous pantomime, getting along nicely with the other, when the pistol case and package of cartridges were discovered. No amount of good German, bad German, emphatic English or frantic gesticulations, would pass this. It had to be taken

2*

out, to the derangement of my packing, and submitted to an officer, who finally passed it, however, after
charging an insignificant sum for duty; and I am
happy to say that it has since been safely delivered
to its destination. Five minutes longer, and I should
have missed the train. I registered an inward vow
never again to bring any deadly weapons to Germany, except such as I was willing to carry on my
own person, and advise all future travelers to come
to a similar determination.

Off at last. We passed rapidly through many
points of interest at which we ought to have stopped, to do justice to the country — such as Hanover,
Brunswick, Magdeburg and Leipsic. At the former
place we changed cars, and had time to obtain an excellent dinner; and there, also, I was taught a lesson
which may be of service hereafter. We took our
hand baggage into a waiting room, whilst we proceeded to an adjoining *Restauration.* With the other
pieces I very carelessly left a valuable gold-headed
cane — valuable intrinsically, as a relic, and as the
gift of a cherished friend. On our return, we found
the articles where we left them, except the cane, and
lo, that was gone! In five minutes the train would
start, and it appeared to be a hopeless case. My companion had a little French and less German. We
seized an official, who might have been either a railway porter or a Field Marshal, for aught we knew to
the contrary, and contrived to make him understand

the loss. He found another officer, went off with him, and returned with the cane, which he put through the window of the coach just as the train was starting. He appeared to be as pleased as I was, and the last I saw of him he was bowing his acknowledgments of the reward I had slipped into his hand. The probability is that some police officer had seen the cane and taken it to a place of safety. I was assured that I could certainly have obtained it, even after weeks of delay, so perfect are the police arrangements in the railway stations of Germany; but I shall not test them in that way again.

Off again. We were still in rather a poor country, and certainly saw but little to note. Lots of peasant women were at work in the fields, doing work which might be good for man or beast, but which it was painful to see them labor at. We had observed already that the management of railways is very different from the American system. Every precaution for safety is enforced, and an accident is rarely heard of. The tracks are enclosed, and men are stationed all along, within sight of each other, to give warning of danger. All the railway buildings are of a very substantial character, and many of them quite imposing in architectural effect, heightened, in most cases, by pretty flowers in the windows, with all ugly angles toned down by the growth of climbing plants.

Not much else did we take note of in our rapid journey. One thing, however, we did learn, viz:

that it is not safe to assume that English speech is not understood in Germany. A very pretty German lady was in the carriage with us, the latter part of the journey. Supposing she did not speak English, my companion and myself talked away quite oblivious of her presence. Suddenly, in the midst of a rather warm discussion about some political question (in which, I may as well admit, the lady carried too many guns for me—for she was, alas! of Boston birth and education!), I effected a diversion by offering a wager that our unknown companion understood every word we said. A hearty laugh from the quiet-looking lady in the corner was the response, and out of that grew a pleasant talk, carried on on her part in the prettiest of not very broken English, in which she admitted that the temptation to laugh at our chatter had been almost too strong to resist many times before my direct reference to her finally gave the finishing touch to her risibilities. Up to this time it had been hard to realize that *we* were "foreigners," but now we began to see it.

So the time was agreeably passed away until we reached our destination, at a little past midnight. We arrived at Dresden in a trifle over thirteen days from New York, including a stop of sixteen hours at Bremen; and here, notwithstanding your anxiety to hear about the war, I shall stop for the present, heartily joining in your wish that my next letter shall be shorter.

II.

DRESDEN, SAXONY, June 16, 1866.

When I finished my last letter, two days ago, all
was quiet in Dresden so far as I could observe or
learn. I supposed it would be at least a week before
I should write you again, and that then my letter
would be chiefly devoted to a description of this place
and of the many wonderful and beautiful things it
contains. I knew you would expect to hear something about the war, and that you would be greatly
surprised to find no interesting particulars thereof
in my last letter. In fact, I took a little malicious
pleasure in your mystification, for I had been thoroughly bewildered myself, not having been able, after
nearly a week of persevering effort, to obtain the
slightest information of a reliable character. Nobody

knew whether Dresden was to be disturbed by either
Prussians or Austrians, and when I asked for some
decided opinion, a shake of the head and a shrug of
the shoulders were the only reply.   One prominent
American gentleman, who has resided here some
years, was decidedly sarcastic on the slowness of the
Germans.   He did not believe they intended to fight
at all.   They would call each other names and shake
their fists, he said, but would never come to blows.*
I think he is rather proud of the tremendous energy
displayed by his countrymen at home, of the brief
time it took for our great war to grow into gigantic
proportions, and the immense amount of blood and
treasure we contrived to spill and spend in four short
years.   He talks of our enormous debt almost as
grandly as though he had furnished all the money
himself, and it seems to me that the confident air he
assumes when he speaks of our ability to pay that
trifle, must help greatly to keep our securities in good
repute in this market.   So satisfied had I become
through his assurances that there would be no trouble, that I had determined to stay out my proposed
visit, and go on quietly about my business of enjoying the sights of this grand old town.   With him, I
thought the Prussian and Austrian armies were like
two angry dogs, growling and bristling and showing

* The wonderful results of the short but bloody campaign which soon
followed, proved how thoroughly mistaken this gentleman was in his
estimate of the German character.   The Prussians, at any rate, were terribly in earnest.

their teeth, but certain to slink away in opposite directions unless some mischievous boy should shy a stick at them and set them on. And I hoped no *enfant terrible* — not even he of France — would be naughty enough to do that.

Well, I had hardly written that letter when all was changed. We could have departed from Dresden any day this week until yesterday, and should have done so but for the vain confidence I have spoken of. But I didn't care to go for a week, and now it looks dubious as to whether anybody can go when they do feel so inclined. In fact, it is doubtful whether my other letter gets through, and it is quite likely you will get this and that together; but as to *when* you will get them I can give no guess.

For it seems that the war has commenced in earnest at last. Yesterday we learned that the Prussians were advancing on this place, and that, by order of the King of Saxony, the railway bridges at Misen and Resea had been destroyed, so as to retard their progress. Railway communication between Dresden and Berlin is thus interrupted, and to-day I hear that trains will stop running to Prague as well. Strangers will therefore have to content themselves here for the present. Yesterday the Saxon troops began to march out of the town, going, it is supposed, to join those of Bavaria, probably in aid of Austria. The movement was kept up all night, and this morning there was not a soldier of the Royal army in town. Dresden, indeed, is abandoned to the Prussians, whose army is expected here this evening. At ten o'clock this morning the King issued a proclamation, which is translated for me as follows:

" To my Faithful Saxons : —

   " An unjust act has obliged me to take up arms.

   " Saxons! because we stand true to the rights of a " brother nation — because we hold fast to the band " which encircles the great German fatherland — be- " cause we do not shrink from our duty to the *Bund* " — we are to be treated as enemies.

   " However painful the sacrifice may be which fate " has ordained for us, let us go cheerfully to the con- " test for the Holy cause.

   " It is true we are small in numbers, but God is " mighty in the weak who trust in him ; and the help " of all who are faithful to the *Bund* will not fail us.

   " Although I am for the moment obliged to lay " down the reins of government and separate myself " from you, I still remain in the midst of my brave " army, where I shall still feel myself in Saxony ; and " hope, when Heaven has blessed our arms, soon to " return to you.

   " I rely firmly on your faithfulness and love. As " we have kept together in the bright hours, so will " we stand together in the hour of trial. Do you " also trust in me, whose highest aim was and is your " welfare.

" With God for the Right.   Let that be our watch-
" word !

" JOHN.

" DRESDEN, 16th June, 1866."

This proclamation is published in an "extra" by
the newspapers, and with it is given the correspondence which took place yesterday between the Prussian Ambassador to the Court of Dresden, Count
Schulenburg, and the Saxon Prime Minister, Baron
von Beust.   The Prussian writes a very insolent letter, demanding that the Saxon army shall be instantly
placed on a peace footing — that Saxony shall follow
the lead of Prussia in withdrawing from the German
Parliament — and that the King shall govern Saxony
according to the reformed system of Prussia.   If Saxony refuses to accede to these demands, the King of
Prussia, "much to his regret," will be obliged to
treat her as an enemy.   Saxony is reminded that,
with her geographical position between the two great
German powers, she cannot hope to remain neutral.

The Saxon Minister replies that Saxony cannot
think of separating from the *Bund*, or of acceding to
either of the other demands of Prussia.

Upon the receipt of this note the Prussian Ambassador returned a formal declaration of war, and at
midnight the Prussian troops marched into Saxony
at Strehla, about thirty-five miles from this place.

This morning King John left Dresden for his army,
his principal ministers accompanying him.   He ap-

pointed a commission in a subsequent proclamation, to govern his possessions during his absence. And now all Dresden is patiently or sullenly expecting the arrival of the Prussians. Unless the Austrians should come as well, of course there will be no fight here, as no resistance will be offered by the Saxons.

John of Saxony is quite aged and infirm. He is greatly beloved by his people, though only about one-fifth of them are of the Roman Catholic religion, like himself. He is a beautiful old man, with one of the most intellectual faces I ever saw. His private character is irreproachable; but not so much can be said, I am told, for his eldest son. The King leads a very quiet life, and is devoted to literary pursuits. A week ago the great majority of his subjects were for Austria. Then it was supposed that the Austrians would get here first. Now, it being certain that Dresden is left to the tender mercies of the Prussians, I observe that many of the citizens think it is not so bad a thing to be a Prussian after all. "We shall all be Prussians to-morrow," said a merchant to me to-day. "You were all Austrians, yesterday," responded I. He shrugged his shoulders in a way that expressed more than I can put into English. They all do that here, quite beyond the power of translation. "What shall we do?" said he. "Our King has left us. We are without a head."

This afternoon a good many Saxon troops marched through the city, coming from the Prussian frontier and retreating before the Prussians probably, to join their brethren who left yesterday and this morning to unite with the Bavarians. I saw them march across the two magnificent bridges over the Elbe, which connect the old and new towns now composing the city of Dresden. It was an imposing sight, and afforded a more vivid idea of the pomp and circumstance of war than we obtained in Buffalo during the whole period of our great rebellion. To-night I hear that there has been a fight not far from this place, and also that the Prussians have seized Hanover and taken its King a prisoner.

Nearly all the smaller German powers voted against Prussia in the *Bund*, and Bismarck has determined to treat such action as a declaration of war against Prussia. No doubt the latter power will overrun those weak states. Many people tell me that it is quite possible I have seen the last of Saxony as an independent Kingdom: I hope not. I know that the King has removed all his private jewels from the place where they were exhibited, and the great Picture Gallery is closed to the public to-day, and its entrances are built up. This is said to be only a precautionary measure against riot by the citizens, whilst the soldiers are away from the garrisons. It seems hardly probable, however, that the citizens would attempt to destroy the priceless treasures in the Gallery, which are justly their greatest pride.

As I said in the beginning, I expected this letter

would be principally devoted to describing the sights of Dresden. It was my intention to give no small portion of it to the Picture Gallery, in which I have spent many hours the past week. But it looks now as though I should have plenty of leisure on my hands for some days to come, so I can postpone that pleasant task till my next.

Being shut up here, you will be glad to hear that I am in good company. There are a great many Americans in Dresden, and Buffalo has quite a representation. Mr. and Mrs. R. J. S. arrived here from the Tyrol, the day after I did; and a day or two later came Mr. and Mrs. G. S. H. and their son, Mr. A. H. They are all here still. We talk about holding a Buffalo Convention. We all find consolation in the thought that if we must be detained we could not find a pleasanter place to stay in, always excepting Buffalo, as a matter of course. Besides Americans, there are but few other foreigners in town, though at this season Dresden is usually full of representatives of all nations. Many Russians and Poles left some time ago, when their money began to depreciate, and the English visitors are nearly all gone also; so we Americans are in the majority. Much of the business of the city is in the sale of goods to foreigners, and the Dresdeners feel their absence very keenly.

If there should be a fight in this vicinity you may have a letter from " Our War Correspondent " on the spot.

III.

OCCUPATION OF DRESDEN BY THE PRUSSIANS. — THE AUS-
TRIANS EXPECTED. — ALARMING RUMORS. — FLIGHT OF
THE TOURISTS. — DIFFICULTIES OF GETTING AWAY, AND
HOW THEY WERE OVERCOME. — ARRIVAL AT BERLIN. —
SIGHT-SEEING THERE AND THEREABOUTS.—"GREENBACKS
ARE GOOD."

BERLIN, June 24, 1866.

Whilst I was writing my last letter the Saxon
troops were marching out of Dresden, and the Prussians were hourly expected to come and take possession. About noon the next day (Monday, June 18th)
they did come, and I was fortunate enough to see the
first of them. Small squads of cavalry were in the
advance, and scoured through the streets, as if they
expected to meet some resistance. They found none,
however, for the citizens had been expecting them
the previous twenty-four hours, and it was hard to
say from appearances that the Prussians were not just
as welcome as the Saxon soldiery had been. In a
very few hours the town was completely occupied by

the invading army. I saw some fifteen thousand
Prussian soldiers march into Dresden, over the great
bridge across the Elbe, and was told that before night
thirty thousand of them were in the city. It was an
exciting scene, one of the most brilliant I ever beheld,
as they passed over that long and magnificent bridge.
The men were splendidly equipped, the horses fine,
and it was altogether more like a great holiday pa-
rade than an act of actual war. Most of the soldiers
had green branches stuck in their hats, and they
laughed and joked with the citizens in a very friendly
way. In fact it was difficult to realize that these
were the soldiers of a power which had just declared
war against the country and were now taking possession of its capital, for the people were apparently
as friendly as the soldiers. The shops were not
closed, nor was business at all interrupted, except
through the curiosity of the citizens. In an hour or
two the Prussians had the palaces and public buildings under guard, and the occupation of Dresden, the
first important hostile act of what may prove a long
and bloody war, was complete.

The Prussian commander, General von Bittenfeld,
and his staff, took quarters at the Hotel Bellevue,
where the American travelers, of whom I wrote you
last week, including the Buffalo party, were stopping;
but the guests were not disturbed in any way. The
General is a fine-looking man of about sixty, with a
thin red face and white hair, a light moustache, and

no beard. He is about five feet ten inches high and stoops slightly. Early the next day he issued a proclamation to the Saxons, telling them that the Prussians had not come as enemies, but as friends, to protect their country against an invasion by a common enemy. It would depend upon the Saxons themselves whether the measures adopted should be mild or severe. They intended to hold the country until the questions between Austria and Prussia should be decided. The tone of the proclamation was calculated to make the Saxon people believe that their best policy would be to unite with the Prussians; and from what I could observe, I came to the conclusion that a majority of the citizens of Dresden were of that opinion, though the Court party and the aristocracy undoubtedly sympathized with the government in taking sides with the Austrians.

It has been said many times by correspondents of English and American newspapers, that the Prussian soldiers were not heartily in favor of this war, and that they would be unwilling to attack the Austrians. I suggested this idea to a prominent Dresden citizen, a strong sympathizer with the Prussians, by the way, in their ambition to become the leading power of the German people. "Not so," replied he, "the Prussians will fight fast enough when they see the white coats (the Austrians). If there ever had been any reluctance to fight, on the part of the Prussians, I imagine it is all dissipated by the address which the Austrian commander-in-chief, Marshal Benedek, has made to his army on taking command. He tells his soldiers that the Prussians pride themselves on the long ranges of their guns, and of their six-shooting rifles, and that they expect great advantages from the use of these weapons. He does not intend to let them gain anything from this. He will bring the fighting to close quarters, where Austrian strength and Austrian bayonets, backed by Austrian bravery, will, as they always have done, gain the day. He promises to lead his men to the capital of the enemy, where they shall repay themselves, *as they choose*, for all the hardships and privations they have endured.

This brutal threat to sack and plunder Berlin, and to leave its inhabitants to the tender mercies of his soldiers, is quite in keeping with the reputation of the Austrian commander, who is said to be a second Haynau. Its effect on the Prussians has certainly been a good one, worth more, perhaps, than any address which could have been published by their own King or General-in-Chief. It was received in Dresden the day after the Prussians took possession of the city, and I fancied I could see that the soldiers appeared more enthusiastic than before.

That day (Tuesday) we heard rumors of fighting in the vicinity, and that the Austrians were advancing in great force. We were advised to get away as early as possible, as the bridges might be destroyed, and then we would perhaps be shut up in Dresden an indefinite length of time. The way was clear by rail to the Prussian capital now, but how long it would remain so no one could tell. It was the only route open from Dresden, also; so, although we should not have gone there had choice been left us, we determined to get ready for a journey to Berlin next day.

When next day came, however, it looked very doubtful whether we could avail ourselves of this last chance. In the morning Dresden was all excitement. All sorts of alarming rumors were in circulation. The Austrians, one hundred thousand strong, were marching toward the city. There had been skirmishing already, and the Prussians had been driven back. There would be fighting in the streets before the day was over. If the Prussians could not hold the city they would destroy it, and blow up the bridges so that the Austrians could not follow them. The Austrians were within two hours' march — one hour's march — in sight — and would be here directly!

As we could not leave till the afternoon at three o'clock, you may imagine that the excitement had become somewhat feverish before that time. Not at all inclined at any time to give credit to wild rumors, I could yet see for myself that the Prussians were preparing for a conflict. They were posted in all the squares and market places, under arms. The shops were being rapidly closed. The soldiers were cutting down the large trees in the Great Garden, and the

3

people in the neighboring houses were warned to leave them. The Austrians were expected to come from that direction. Droschkies and carriages, usually to be seen everywhere, were now not to be had for love or money. Finally, though my trunks had been packed for hours, I began to think we should not get away after all.

Fortunately, a friend, a resident of Dresden, was as anxious on our account as we were ourselves. After an hour's search he procured us a carriage, and we started for the railway station, which is in the new town, not at all sure that we would find the great railway bridge, over which we had to drive, still standing. At the last moment, as the last trunk was being carried out, our friend, who is a nervous, excitable man, whispered that he had something to tell me, but would not tell it until we were all in the carriage. "What is it?" asked I, as I took my seat. He wrung my hand and whispered that he had just heard the Prussians were mistaken — they were expecting the Austrians from one direction, but they were coming, "a hundred thousand of them!" that way — pointing to the direction in which we were going. "But," he added, "perhaps you will be off before they arrive. God bless you!" I thought this was a comforting assurance to start away on, but it was not the last. My friend (perfectly in earnest, I am sure, only he is the most excitable creature I ever met) stopped the carriage to tell me something more.

"I almost forgot," he gasped. "For God's sake don't tell your wife. If you get to Berlin get out again as quick as you can. They have got the cholera there awfully! Good-bye."

With this pleasant prospect before us, we started; drove over the bridge and into the station all right, passing thousands of travelers, it seemed, hurrying away from the city. At the station we found our Buffalo friends, and many other Americans, who, like ourselves, had got there with difficulty. One lady, not unknown where this will be read, had displayed a degree of American energy and coolness under trying circumstances, which deserves to be mentioned. As no carriages were to be had, most of the party had walked from the hotel to the station, more than a mile. The lady of whom I speak was not able to do this, and there was much anxiety to know how she could be taken there. She proved equal to the emergency, however. There was a carriage at the hotel door, waiting for some one who had been lucky enough to secure it. Not another could be had at any price. What then does this lady do? She coolly stepped into the carriage, and, saying "*eisenbahn!*" to the driver, left the event to fate. The poor driver was voluble, almost frantic, in his remonstrances. The carriage was not for her! Would not the lady please get out? The lady understood never a syllable of what he said, and had only one German word to give back. "*Eisenbahn, eisenbahn!*" she repeated.

The driver looked desperate, and apparently medi-
tated lifting her out of the carriage. But she was no
feather-weight, as was plain to be seen, and if such
an energetic plan occurred to him he did not attempt to carry it out. At length the poor fellow,
with a despairing shrug, abandoned the argument,
mounted the box, and drove at a great pace down to
the railway station, where the lady arrived triumphant, passing several of her friends on the way. Did
not her one German word stand her in good stead
that day? She could not have done so well if she
had had the whole German dictionary at her tongue's
end. This is what her friends told me about the matter: I only tell the story as it was told to me.

At three o'clock the train started, and at half-past
eight in the evening, after a very pleasant ride, we
reached Berlin, where we are all stopping at the *Hotel du Nord*. On the way hither we passed many
Prussian soldiers, *en route* to Dresden, it appeared.
The stations were all strongly guarded, but we met
with no detentions. I think I may assert, however,
for one and all, that when we found ourselves com-
fortably located, although we had not desired to
come, we felt " it was good to be here."

It seems fated that I am not to tell you anything
of Dresden itself, of the glories of its picture-galler-
ies, its museums, its treasures and precious stones,
and the magnificence of its public buildings, though I
saw much of all these during my first week there. I

found time to select a large set of copies of the gems of the Gallery by the great photographer Hanfstaengl — else I should have had but very little, except in memory, to remind me of Dresden. I had intended to make many little excursions from that place, particularly into Saxon Switzerland, and I meant to gossip of these trips, through you, to my friends. Inexorable war has disappointed me, however, and it seems likely to keep me from talking of what it did permit me to see, so much space does it demand for itself. Besides, I want to bring our adventures up to date in this letter, and, therefore, I must content myself with a promised indulgence in some Reminiscences of Dresden, when more time and more space are at my disposal.

Berlin, though a great deal larger, is not nearly so interesting a city as Dresden, nor has it anything like so many objects of attraction, either in itself or in its vicinity. Located in the midst of a flat, uninviting and miserably poor country, it is entirely indebted to Art and History for whatever of beauty or interest it possesses. I shall not trouble you with many particulars about the place, doubting not that they are in general as familiar to you as to myself. I shall only speak of what I see and hear, and shall, I dare say, mix up news about the war with other matters, just as they occur to me. When you wish to learn more about a place than I write, refer to Murray's Hand-Books, which I find in the main quite reliable.

The most conspicuous feature of Berlin is the multitude of statues which are everywhere visible. In all the public squares, on the bridges, on most of the large buildings, private as well as public, statues and groups of sculpture meet the eye. Even humble and unpretentious structures are in this way adorned. The glory of the city, in this respect, is the great equestrian statue of Frederick the Great, modelled by Rauch, and erected in 1851. This is a wonderful piece of work, at once massive, elaborate and beautiful. It is said to be the grandest monument in Europe, and indeed one cannot well conceive how anything in that way can be finer. "Murray" gives a very accurate description of it, but it would occupy too much space to transfer to your columns, and yet anything more brief would not convey a correct idea of this triumph of Art. It is a history, as well as a monument, of Prussia's greatest hero.

Next in importance to this work, and almost as highly esteemed by the Prussians, is the Car of Victory on the top of the Brandenburg Gate, which is at the end of the principal street, considered one of the finest in Europe, called *Unter den Linten*, from a double avenue of lime trees which form a shady walk in the centre for an immense length, a carriage road being on either side. The Car of Victory was carried as a trophy to Paris by Napoleon, but was recovered by the Prussians after the battle of Waterloo, and is probably more highly esteemed by them than ever.

We have made the most of the time the last three days in visiting the sights of the city. We have had drives through the *Thiergarten*, a sort of Central Park without any of its natural beauties ; — a visit to " Kroll's," the greatest place of resort in the city, being an immense garden containing an opera house, at which we heard " La Sonnambula " very well per- formed, and after that an outdoor concert by an or- chestra of more than fifty performers, the promenades in the meantime crowded with well-dressed people, hundreds of little tables in arbors and about the grounds, at nearly every one of which little parties were taking refreshments; the entire place brilliantly illuminated when night came on, with thousands of colored lamps and jets of gas in fanciful and beauti- ful devices, lights darting from fountains, trees and flowers, in most unexpected places, the whole making a fairy scene quite beyond my powers of description; — a drive to Charlottenburg, about three miles from Berlin, our object being to see the famous monument of Queen Louisa, the wife of the late King, which is in a small Doric temple at the extremity of a long walk shaded with fir trees, and is a work of inexpres- sible beauty, considered the masterpiece of Rauch; — a visit to the Royal Porcelain Manufactory, where we saw the whole process of making the elegant wares for which the establishment is famous, and learned that it was founded by Frederick the Great, who cap- tured the artists from Dresden and imprisoned them

here until the work reached a degree of perfection as
high as it had attained in that place; — a visit to the
Zoological Gardens, a place so immense (about eighty
acres) that the really fine collection makes but little
show; — a pilgrimage to the tomb of Humboldt, at
Tegel, the family estate, about nine miles from the
city, a beautiful place, where we sat under the great
oak which was the favorite seat of the philosopher,
and plucked a leaf or two of ivy from his grave.

I have said nothing of our visits to the Museum
and Picture Gallery, and, indeed, have made only the
briefest mention, as you will see, where I might have
written pages with less trouble and more satisfaction
(at least to myself) if I did not limit the space to be
occupied. This style of description cannot be interesting to the general reader, but you must remember
what I said at the beginning of my first letter, viz:
that I was writing more for private friends than for
general readers, and hold me excused accordingly.
Incidents are particularly scarce you will notice, for
to narrate incidents takes up room, and room I have
not to spare. But I will give you one which surprised me some, mortified me more, and yet amused
me a little. I was in an exchange office, getting some
money changed. Two girls came in, one of them de-
siring to sell a bill which she had received from an
American gentleman, she said. It was a $2 bill of a
Michigan bank broken nearly twenty years ago!
They had hardly left before an honest-looking man

came in — a poor shop-keeper I fear — with what he supposed were two $5 greenbacks. They were nothing but advertisements, making no pretence to be money, but printed in a sort of rude imitation of our popular currency, and bearing the legend, in great staring letters, " GREENBACKS ARE GOOD! " and then telling the place *where* greenbacks were good *in exchange for ready-made clothing !* The poor man declared that he had received the bills as good American money. If such rascally tricks as these are common, can it be wondered at that our paper money is in such bad odor abroad ?

Last night there was official intelligence here that the rumors of the defeat of the Prussians in several skirmishes near Dresden are false, and that the Prussian soldiers in Dresden had sacked the residence of the Saxon Prime Minister, Baron von Beust, to whose influence they attributed the action of Saxony in siding with the Austrians. The night before last a fine-looking regiment of soldiers left this place for Leipsic, marching directly under my window. The Government has called out the Reserve and the first *Landwehr*, the latter movement alone giving Prussia one hundred and thirty thousand more effective soldiers, all of whom have served in the army. Unpopular as Bismarck undoubtedly is with the people now, if Prussia is successful in this war he will, perhaps, become the popular idol. It is expected now that he will make concessions to the people, and allow the Parlia-

3*

ment to meet, though the same members whom he has kicked out three times before are sure to be returned again at the forthcoming election. In that case the necessary supplies will be promptly voted, and the Prussian people will be a unit in the war against Austria.

I expect to write you next week from some city on the Rhine.

P. S.—There is no cholera here, I am credibly informed, except amongst the very poor, who are almost starving on account of the high price of provisions, owing to the scarcity produced by the war. Misery like this always attends the strife for glory in Europe.

•

IV.

SIGHT-SEEING IN BERLIN.—THE ROYAL STABLES.—THE GREAT
PALACE.—THE EXCHANGE.—POTSDAM AND ITS SIGHTS.—
COLOGNE, AND THE JOURNEY THITHER.—THE CATHEDRAL.
—OLD STORIES, OLD CHURCHES AND OLD SMELLS.—THE
RHINE.—AN INCIDENT.—THE WAR AND RUMORS OF WAR.

COLOGNE, July 1st, 1866.

If it is as great a bore to read my letters as it is to
write them, I pity such of your subscribers, dear
Commercial, as do me the honor to wade through
them. The fact is, I am sorry that I ever commenced
this series of letters for your columns, for notwithstanding my distinct avowal at the outset of entire
freedom to continue or stop them as I pleased, a
life-long habit of completing whatever I begin, urges
me to go on now, whilst the desire for one day of real
rest after a week of travel and sight-seeing makes this
regularly recurring task a task to be dreaded. Besides, the more I think about it the more conscious I
become of how little that is new or interesting I shall
be able to present you. If I hear of any incident in

the war, the English and French newspapers will be
sure to reach you with the news before my letter can;
and as for what I see in my travels, all has been told
a thousand times before, and each time a thousand
times better than I can tell it, which multiplies the
chances against me fearfully. "Perseverance," however, being my great virtue (if I have one), I will go
on, in spite of such discouraging considerations, with
these rambling, disjointed epistles.

We spent four or five days more in Berlin after I
mailed my last letter, but did not see many of the
sights of the city in that time. One of the days being
"election day," most of the public buildings were
closed, and another being a "fast day," proclaimed by
the King, who invoked the prayers of the people for
the success of the Prussian army, all business was
suspended, and no entrance could be effected into any
of the places most worthy of a visit. An inspection
of the Royal stables, and a visit to the Great Palace,
comprise nearly all I have additional to note of Berlin. It appeared to me that the Royal stud was a
vast concern, and I thought the collection of noble-
looking horses could hardly be excelled, in extent or
value; but I was assured that the stables of the King
of Hanover were much finer in every way. One sec-
tion of the Berlin establishment housed between forty
and fifty coal-black stallions, every one of which
looked to me like a horse of price. In another department were splendid bay carriage-horses, and in

another the Queen's saddle-horses, numerous enough, I should think, to give her a fresh one every day in the month. The state carriages were uncovered and opened for our inspection, and very magnificent were some of them, and very comfortable were others. The official who escorted us was a grand-looking personage, but he did not disdain to accept the fee which, we were told, it was customary to offer him. I find that though nearly all the great palaces of Germany can be entered without payment, it is very difficult to effect an exit without dropping something into various expectant hands ready at every door. In fact, I think it may be laid down as a rule for foreign visitors not to fear giving offence by offering a gratuity to anybody at these places — only be sure and make it large enough.

The Royal Palace is an imposing edifice, vast in size and grand in its surroundings. In the spacious court-yard stands a magnificent group in bronze, by Kiss, representing St. George and the Dragon; a noble work of art, quite equal if not superior to his famous Amazon and Tiger. We were escorted through the Palace by the *castellan*, and the gentlemen of the party were invited to slip their feet into huge list slippers before they could set foot on the polished inlaid wood floors. The different apartments of the Palace are sumptuously, some of them gorgeously, furnished; but I will not undertake a description of them. The " White Hall " struck me as the

most magnificent of all. This room is fitted entirely
with silver and white decorations. In it are statues
of the twelve Brandenburg Electors, and allegorical
figures representing the Prussian provinces. It is
lighted by a superb chandelier, of silver and cut-glass
and crystal, which holds between two and three thousand candles. There are many fine and extremely
interesting portraits in the different rooms. But the
crowning glory of the Palace, to my thinking, is the
beautiful Chapel, which was built and decorated between the years 1848 and 1854. The dome is peculiarly grand, and the paintings and frescoes, to me,
were miracles of art. The King does not live in this
grand Palace, preferring to live in a smaller one near
by, which was his home as Crown Prince. I dare say
he is much more comfortable where he is; certainly
the building has a more home-like look.

A peculiarity, and certainly not a pleasing peculiarity, of most of the large buildings I have yet seen in
Germany, is that they are covered with stucco, a
fact which is due I suppose to the scarcity of stone
fit for building purposes. In Berlin nearly all the
buildings, including the palaces, are built of a coarse
kind of brick, and plastered with this stucco. An exception to this rule, however, is the Exchange, or
Bourse, which is a very noble building of light brown
stone, the walls and pillars of the interior being entirely of polished granite and marble. I have never
seen any edifice more solidly constructed, or better

adapted to its object. It was built quite recently by a company composed of members of the Exchange, and cost about a million of dollars.

We spent two days in Potsdam, which is a town of about forty thousand inhabitants, twenty miles from Berlin. It is a city of palaces, containing four or five Royal residences, and is a very interesting place. Two very hard days' work may be done in sight-seeing here. We visited the Church of the Garrison, where we saw the plain metal sarcophagus which holds the remains of the Great Frederick; Sans Souci, which was built by him to suit his own taste, but which certainly suits no one else, and where he and Voltaire had their friendly and unfriendly disputes; the famous Windmill which Frederick wished to buy but could not, and about which he sustained one of the few defeats of his career, *in a law suit;* the New Palace which he built in a fit of bravado, to show his enemies that his finances were not exhausted by the tremendous expenditures of the seven years' war — an immense building of red brick, with flat white marble pillars, a most comfortless-looking structure, more like a great factory or barracks than a Royal residence, the walls and ceilings of one apartment lined with minerals and shells in singularly bad taste, like nothing ever seen before, except in a " spectacle piece " in a theatre; the Raphael Hall, which contains copies, good, bad and indifferent, of most of the paintings and cartoons of the divine master; the gardens

of Prince Carl, which are laid out with the most exquisite taste and afford many charming views; and,
finally, we visited Babelsberg, a modern castle of white
brick, built by the present king, and as charming a
residence as it is possible to conceive, the grounds,
gardens, terraces, fountains and walks being more
beautiful than anything of the kind we had hitherto
seen.   This last is the most like a "home" of any royal
residence in Germany, for, elegant as are all its furn-
ishings and surroundings, it does not strike one as
being too grand for everyday life.   It has an air of
comfort about it quite refreshing after witnessing the
cold, stately and cheerless grandeur of the other palaces.   Here the Princess Royal of England, the next
Queen of Prussia in all probability, spent her honey-
moon, and we saw in her apartments several specimens of her water-color drawings, which might well
be mistaken for the work of a professed master of the
art.

Potsdam is a dull, though a very beautiful, place.
It has only one or two hotels worthy the name, and
those not large ones; but we found the charges quite
as large as the most pretentious establishments could
make up.   We left the place on the evening of the
28th, bound per rail for Cologne, where we arrived
next morning, after a very tedious and fatiguing ride.
Thirteen hours' journey on the railway is a longer
stretch than I would advise any traveler for pleasure
in this country to take, for it is hardly possible but

he must pass through places where he might profitably stop a day or so. We passed through several such, notably Magdeburg, a city of eighty thousand inhabitants, and a fortress of the first class, memorable for its long resistance of several sieges in the Thirty Years' War, and for its capture, after two years' siege, by Tilly, who carried it by assault and slaughtered thirty thousand of its inhabitants without distinction of age or sex; Brunswick, a very ancient and picturesque town of forty thousand people, the capital of the Duchy of the same name, containing many objects worthy of the tourist's attention; Hanover, a beautiful city with a population of seventy thousand, who pride themselves on speaking the purest German; the old town of Minden, where the famous battle was fought; and Dusseldorf, with its celebrated school of painting. At all these places we should have been glad to linger a little while, but we were anxious to reach the Rhine as quickly as possible, not knowing how soon the chances of war might put a stop to our progress.

I find a note made on leaving Potsdam (emphasize the last syllable) of nearly six dollars in gold paid for extra baggage; yet there were but three not very heavy pieces for two and a half passage tickets. Fancy paying such a sum between Buffalo and New York — a journey of about the same length — where as much baggage has always been allowed for two passengers. What growling there would be!

Here, in this venerable old town of Cologne (spelt Cöln, pronounced *Keln*, by the Germans), this is the third day of our sojourn. It is the most ancient and quaint-looking place I have ever seen, and the wonder to me is that the Guide-Books make so little account of it. Its Cathedral, alone, is worth a long journey to see. The history and appearance of this noble pile were tolerably familiar to me before I saw it — as they are also, doubtless, to most readers — but I was more than surprised by the reality, after all. Though begun in the thirteenth century, the plan of the old architect is hardly more than half completed. The two principal towers were to be five hundred feet high. The one upon which people are now at work is less than a fourth of that height. This is the new tower — the old one, on which but little has been done for centuries, is about one hundred and seventy feet high, and will have to be greatly repaired if the structure is ever completed, age or defective material having caused most of the fine work to crumble away. There is much hope that the present generation will see the original design carried out, the last two Kings of Prussia having taken deep interest in the work, and contributed very liberally toward it. An association has been established, having branches in all parts of Europe, for the purpose of collecting funds in behalf of this object. I saw, in the Museum, many pictures offered for sale, contributed by the artists for completing the Cathedral. If it ever is finished what a monument of Gothic architecture it will be, and what a pity it is that the name of its great designer has been lost! Every visitor is afforded the opportunity to give something toward the great work: I hope no one fails to avail himself of it.

Cologne is so old a city that its early history is lost in obscurity. Some idea of its antiquity may be formed from the fact that Agrippina, the mother of Nero, was born here, and that in the year 508, Clovis was here declared King of the Franks. Old as it is, it looks its age every day of it, and it *smells* older yet. I think some of the original scents of the ancient Romans must be preserved to this day. And I saw old women crawling about the streets who might have been the mothers of its founders. As we passed out of the Church of St. Ursula and the Eleven Thousand Virgins, we came upon an old crone so withered and so hideous that I would have believed her at once if she had asserted that she was one of the Eleven Thousand, spared by the barbarians on account of her remarkable ugliness. In this old church the bones and skulls of the Eleven Thousand Virgins are preserved, packed with horrible ingenuity into the walls, so that the church may be said to be lined with them. Many niches and open spaces are left, filled with the bones and covered with glass; the ghastly relics are thus visible everywhere to the eye, forming an exhibition as strange as it is disgusting. The legend is that St. Ursula (supposed to be a Princess of Britany) and her

virgin train, on their return from a pilgrimage to
Rome, were slaughtered at Cologne by the Huns, because they refused to break their vows of chastity.
In one little room, called the Golden Chamber, the
skulls of a good many of the more favored companions of the sainted Ursula are preserved. They are
encased in silver, and arranged on shelves, looking
more like a lot of heathen fetishes or gods than the
heads of pretty Christian virgins. Eleven thousand
is rather a staggering number, certainly, but I should
think I saw bones enough to make that many skele-
tons, and if they are not the remains of the Virgins
no one knows what they are, and therefore I am determined to pin my faith to the legend. We were
shown many other curious relics in that Golden
Chamber, among others one of the stone jars in
which the water was turned into wine at the Marriage in Cana. No one should doubt the authenticity
of the stories about these relics, because, if you do,
you see, away goes all the interest in looking at
them!

There are several other curious old churches in Cologne. One, St. Gereon's, begun in 1066, is lined
with the bones of six thousand martyrs slain on this
spot during the persecution of Diocletian. They are
rather proud of their old bones, it appears, in the
Churches here. Another, the Apostles' Church, begun in 1020, has one of the lightest and pleasantest
interiors which it is possible to conceive, notwith-

standing its great age. Another, the Church of St. Peter, is chiefly noted from containing as its altarpiece, a famous painting by Rubens, representing the crucifixion of that sturdy old apostle, with his head downward. It is only a copy which the visitors see until a fee of about half-a-dollar is paid to the sacristan; then the frame is swung round, exposing on the back the great original. It is a wonderful picture, of course, but by no means a pleasant thing to look at notwithstanding. It is said that Rubens regarded it as his best work.

But the interesting features of Cologne are by no means limited to its churches. One might wander for days about its crooked and narrow old streets, and still find something to interest him, though I think he would need plenty of the *Eau de Cologne* to reconcile his nose to the task. I saw streets so narrow — if, indeed, they could be called streets — that people could shake hands from the upper windows of the houses on opposite sides. The city is built on the left bank of the Rhine, going down, and is connected with the opposite shore by a bridge of boats which opens to let vessels pass through, and by a magnificent iron railway bridge, under which steamers can pass. Though I date my letter from Cologne we are stopping on the right bank, exactly opposite, at the *Hotel Bellevue*, which affords a magnificent view of Cologne. This place is called Deutz, and is to Cologne what Brooklyn is to New York, only much nearer. Here we have more than all the advantages of a stay in the larger city, and are away from its vile smells.

The classic Rhine flows rapidly between these two places, and the scene presents an ever-varying panorama of remarkable beauty. I enjoyed a swim in the river yesterday, but witnessed a sight this morning which will prevent my repeating the experiment, as I had intended to do before I go away. Leaning over the garden wall of the hotel, and looking up the stream, I saw a boat coming toward me in which were two men. They had something in tow — I could not make out what it was — floating behind the boat. People were following on the shore, and, as the boat neared where I was, an official stopped them at a point above where it was to land. Two men came along carrying a stretcher, and then, suddenly, the scene in the opening chapter of "Our Mutual Friend" was realized to me. The dead body of a man who had been drowned while bathing three days before was floated to the shore, placed upon the stretcher, and carried away. It was a horrible incident, which I should have avoided the sight of, had I known what it was a moment earlier than I did.

I think we leave this city to-morrow, bound up the Rhine, but with no settled plans as to stopping places, for the war may bring us to a sudden halt at any point. I wish I could give you some news of the war which would be interesting, but I cannot. On the evening of the 29th a salute was fired at the fort adjoining this house, on account of the victory which the Prussians claim at the late battle in Bohemia. I observe that the Austrians claim the victory also: perhaps both were whipped. The latter power has certainly given the Italians a severe repulse in Venetia. But I will give you no particulars of either affair, knowing you will get them from the same source that I would, and in advance of this. It appears that the conflict is widening, and it is hardly possible that any German power, or France either for that matter, will be able to maintain neutrality. The result will be a good one, I hope: the wiping out of all the petty German potentates, and the consolidation of all Northern Germany under Prussian rule, and of all Southern Germany under Austrian dominion. If Italy succeeds in securing Venetia, and France does not get any of the Rhine country, the world should be satisfied, I think. This would be rather hard on the poor little Dukes and Kings, but the better for mankind.

One of our party was in Berlin a day later than we were, when the news of the battle was received there. The excitement and enthusiasm were immense. The King came out and spoke to the crowd, and was loudly cheered. But Bismarck was the hero of the hour. When he appeared, the scene became an ovation, and the moment must have been a proud and happy one for him. It is *his* war: his political fortunes are staked upon the result. If Prussia succeeds, he will become a national idol, second only to the great Frederick. If Austria wins, woe to Bismarck. In any event, I believe the Prussian people are sure to secure a freer and better government than they have hitherto enjoyed; and if this is the result in North Germany, Austria will hardly be able to maintain her despotic sway.

Speaking of our party: it is a pretty large one — sixteen Americans in all, who were in Dresden together a week, were together in the flight from that place, and have been together ever since. There is so little travel in Germany this season that we leave a large vacancy at all the hotels when we go away. We find it quite pleasant to keep together. One party contributes a little German, another a little French, and all have plenty of vigorous English at command; so we get along nicely. We may take different routes soon, but I think each of us hopes that we shall all meet again.

Meanwhile, good-bye for the present.

V.

LAST WORDS ABOUT COLOGNE. — THE "SERVICE" NUISANCE.
—A TRIP UP THE RHINE AND A RAPID GLANCE AT SOME
OF ITS FAMOUS PLACES. — WIESBADEN, ITS WATERS AND
ITS HELL. — FRANKFORT AND HOMBURG. — THE WAR EX-
CITEMENT.—ARRIVAL AT HEIDELBERG.

HEIDELBERG, July 8th, 1866.

I mailed my last letter at Cologne, of which fragrant old town we took leave the day following. Before speaking of our trip up the Rhine, however, I am moved to say a few last words about Cologne. It is, as I said in my last, an exceedingly interesting city, but, as far as my experience goes, one of the most expensive places at which the traveler can sojourn. In respect to the charges for admission to "sights," it reminds one strongly of Niagara Falls, as that place used to be when a "quarter" was demanded by some-body every time one turned around. We found the hotel charges, too, higher here than at any other city we had visited, though, it must be admitted, the fare and attendance were better than usual.

4

Here, I bethink me, would be as good a place as any to ease my mind upon a point which has been felt, I am sure, by every American traveler in Germany. I allude to the annoyance to which one is subjected at leaving a hotel, by the array of servants who waylay him upon the stairs, in the hall, and at the carriage door, all expectant of a fee, and all plainly expressing their feelings, at least by looks and shrugs, if they are disappointed. To be obliged to run the gauntlet of this hungry throng is an ordeal more to be dreaded than packing of trunks, or any other unpleasant incidents which alloy the pleasures of traveling. And it is the more annoying from the fact that one has only a few minutes before found a good round charge for "service" at the end of every day's items in his hotel bill. "Oh, lord," said one of our party to me recently, as we drove away from a hotel, "I shall die of this before I get to Switzerland! I can't get used to it. I don't want to appear mean, and yet I don't want to be imposed upon — but it is wearing me to a shadow!" She was exhausted and out of breath, but found it again when I asked what was the matter. "The matter!" she exclaimed. "Why, these servants — they will be the death of me. I thought I would be systematic about it this time. I paid the *portier* and the head waiter when I ordered my bill. Then I rung for the chambermaid and paid her. Then I sent for the little smooth-faced waiter, who had been so polite to me, and paid him liberally.

These were the only servants who had done anything for me, except the man who handled my trunks, and him I expected to pay at the last moment, and flattered myself he would be the last. But what do you suppose that treacherous little villain — the smooth-faced smiling little villain of a waiter — did? I had given him a thaler, but was he grateful? No. He got a lot of other servants who had never shown their faces since I had been in the house, and when I left my room there they were in the hall, all in a row, bowing and scraping to me, and wishing me 'much pleasure.' There were so many of them that I had not change enough left to give each something — so I could only thank them and return their bows. At last I rushed away, my face all in a blaze, and jumped into the carriage, forgetting, in my desperation, to pay the baggage man after all! Oh, it is dreadful, dreadful!"

I have no doubt this lady's description of her experience will be recognized and corroborated by all travelers in Europe who may chance to see it. I could say more upon the subject, but it is a more than twice-told tale, and I will therefore end it here.

We had picked out from the advertisement of a " *Rhein-Dampfschiff-fahrt* " (so in the vernacular, and mind you spell it right), the name of the little steamer we had to take, and at ten o'clock were on board. Then began our trip " Up the Rhine," that beautiful river whose charms have been so often sung,

and so well sung that I am afraid to even join in the
chorus.   What I do venture to say, therefore, of our
trip, shall have at least the merit of brevity.   For
many miles after we left Cologne I think there was a
general feeling of disappointment in our party.   The
scenery was beautiful, it is true, but it lacked those
grand and romantic features which we had been
taught to expect.   Our own noble Hudson was remembered with pride, and we thought that glorious
river only needed to be as well known to be as loudly
sung and as universally admired as the classic Rhine.
As the first day wore on, however, this somewhat
dissatisfied state of mind disappeared; the scenery
became grander, more like what we had imagined it
would be, and before we landed at Coblenz, in the
evening, all were willing to admit that the day had
been one of surprising enjoyment, and that such a
magnificent panorama of scenery as we had been passing for hours, was not anywhere else to be seen: not
even in America.

Yet it must be admitted that much of the charm
that belongs to the Rhine is due to the legends and
romances which add an interest to every crag and
mountain and ruin along its banks.   Grand as is the
view at every bend of the noble river — picturesque
as are the ruins which stud every mountain slope —
the stories of old-time romance are necessary to the
completeness of the picture, and there is no crag
or mountain or ruin without such a story.   I had

thought to transcribe these stories for you — or at least such of them as most interested me — but time and space alike forbid. I am quite satisfied that the limit to which I confine myself is too contracted for the purpose, even if I had the skill to arrange the material, which is so embarrassingly abundant, into a pleasing shape. I comfort myself with the thought that my letters may be useful for what they do not tell — that is, they may, from their very poverty of description, induce my readers to look elsewhere for what is not to be found in them. I shall at least show others how *not* to write up the Rhine.

I will just tantalize you a little, though, with the names of a few of the memorable places we passed in our two days' trip up the river. First, after leaving Cologne, came Bonn, an old town of near twenty thousand inhabitants, with a great University at which the late Prince "Albert the Good" was a student; a Cathedral which is surmounted by five towers, and was founded by Helena the mother of Constantine the Great, a fact which will give you an idea of its antiquity; in the vicinity are many interesting objects to attract the tourist, amongst them a little chapel on the summit of the mountain, containing the sacred stairs of Pilate's Judgment Hall, still bearing the stains of the blood which fell from the Saviour's brow, caused by the Crown of Thorns! No one is allowed to ascend these stairs except on bended knees.

Soon after, we pass the Seven Mountains, the most interesting of the group being "The Castled Crag of Drachenfels," so beautifully described by Byron:

"The castled crag of Drachenfels
    Frowns o'er the wide and winding Rhine,
Whose breast of waters broadly swells
    Between the banks which bear the vine;
And hills all rich with blossom'd trees,
    And fields which promise corn and wine,
And scattered cities crowning these,
    Whose far white walls along them shine,
Have strew'd a scene which I should see
With double joy wert *thou* with me."

Here we ought to have stopped at least a day, so many points of interest are there in the neighborhood which the traveler ought to explore; but inexorable haste forbade this, and the little steamer carried us along, past the Castle of Rolandseck, where Roland, a nephew of Charlemagne, lived a hermit for many years, in sight of the Convent of Nonnenworth within whose walls his betrothed bride had taken the veil on hearing a false report of his death. This story is the subject of one of Schiller's most beautiful ballads. In rapid succession we pass old villages — wonderfully small of their age; more "castled crags" and terraced hills; indeed, we are fairly tired out with looking at the places famous in song and story which are strung together on the banks of the Rhine, all the way to Coblenz, where we stop for the night.

Coblenz is quite an important old town, strongly

fortified, the capital of the Rhenish provinces of Prussia. Here the Moselle enters the Rhine, and directly opposite is the famous fortress of Ehrenbreitstein, the Gibraltar of the Rhine, a work of wonderful strength and as picturesque as it is strong. It is said the Prussians are constantly adding to the strength and resources of this fortress. Just now they are especially active, and strangers are not allowed to inspect the place. Coblenz is a very nice town to lose oneself in, and some of our party did not fail to avail themselves of the opportunity in the evening. Another river, the Lahn, pours its waters into the Rhine at Coblenz, and the trade of the three rivers adds much to the business of the town. It is the great centre of the trade in the Rhine and Moselle wines. One merchant's cellars are so wide and lofty that a stage-coach loaded might easily drive round in them.

I must not, however, occupy my space with particulars which can be found in "Murray," unless I wish to keep you on the Rhine longer than I was — which I do not. We left Coblenz the next morning, and soon found that we had the most interesting part of the Rhine yet to see. I have no language to describe its beauties. I find notes of the Stolzenfels castle, where Isabella, sister of Henry III. of England and bride of the Emperor Frederick II., was lodged with a splendid retinue in 1235; the castle of Lahneck, of which Goethe sung in his verses, "Geister Gruss;" Boppart, a town built by the Romans;

the twin castles of Sternberg and Liebenstein, built
by two brothers who were in love with the same
lady, the legend says, and a very sad legend it is;
the fortress of Rheinfels, the most extensive ruin on
the Rhine, built on a rock three hundred and sixty-
eight feet above the river; the castle of Schönberg
(Beautiful Hill), which received its name, according
to the story, from seven beautiful but hard-hearted
daughters of the house, who turned the heads of all
the young knights but would not marry any of them,
and were therefore changed into seven rocks, still to
be seen when the water is low; the old castle of Stah-
leck, which was the seat of the Electors Palatine till
the middle of the thirteenth century; the castle of
Rheinstein, which has been restored as near as possible to its original condition, and is now a summer
residence of Prince Frederick of Prussia; the little
square Mouse Tower, to which the wicked Bishop
Hatto fled in vain from the rats, after he had burned
up the poor famished people who had come into his
barn on his promise to give them corn —

> " ' I' faith 'tis an excellent bonfire ! ' quoth he,
> 'And the country is greatly obliged to me
> For ridding it, in these times forlorn,
> Of rats that only consume the corn.' "

You, and all my readers, are doubtless familiar with
Southey's splendid poetical version of the legend —
how the next day a servant came to tell the Bishop

that the rats had devoured all his corn — how another
came to bid him fly, " ten thousand rats are coming
this way!"— how he did fly to this tower, and how
the rats followed him there, " in at the window, and
in at the door," thousands and thousands of them :—

> " They have whetted their teeth against the stones,
> And now they pick the Bishop's bones;
> They gnaw'd the flesh from every limb,
> For they were sent to do justice on him."

There was nothing about the appearance of the
Mouse Tower to attract attention. A queer little
tower, like a thick chimney poking out of the water,
we should have passed it without notice if we had not
been constantly on the look-out, guide book in hand,
for memorable places. And so with many other objects of which we have all heard: it should be frankly
admitted that the legend, song or story gave the im-
pulse to look for them. It was a showery day, this
last of ours on the Rhine, and there was a constant
running out of the cabin on the little steamer to look
at some famous spot, and running in again to get out
of the wet. Little groups gathered to listen to the
story of " the next place to look at " (for there was
one in the party who read well — and well she knew
it), whilst some one who cared not for the rain (or
the reading, either, I fear), kept watch, and gave notice when the boat brought us in sight of the spot.
Now and then, as we stopped at a venerable old

4*

town, some would run on shore "just to say they had been in " such and such a place. So we went to " Bingen on the Rhine," and so we went to many other famous places which we saw that day on the glorious river. It would only aggravate you, no less than myself, were I to barely enumerate them. As we passed the hills where grow the precious wines of Rudesheim and Johannisberg — the latter an es- tate belonging to Prince Metternich, the vineyard containing only sixty acres — we could only marvel as we thought how much wine is produced from this little patch, if all the labels are true! Happy is the man who gets a taste of the genuine.

Shortly after passing Johannisberg the banks of the Rhine become less interesting. The country begins to grow flat, and passengers for pleasure seldom as- cend further than Mayence, a few miles above. Our party left the river at Biberich, very near Johannis- berg, and took carriages for Wiesbaden, where we arrived at about eight o'clock in the evening, quite satisfied that we had not half "done" the Rhine. Pray accept this confession that my description of what we did "do" is a still smaller moiety of that. If the reader is half as dissatisfied with it as the writer is, I feel sympathy for him.

But though we spent only two days on the river, we were, I am happy to say, some time longer in the Rhine country. Wiesbaden is between three and four miles from the river. Here we stayed two days, long enough to see the place pretty thoroughly. It is the capital of the Duchy of Nassau, and has about twenty thousand inhabitants. Its mineral waters and baths are among the most celebrated on the continent, and thirty thousand visitors during the season are attracted hither, ostensibly in search of health, but many of them in reality come to gamble. The "hell" is one of the most extensive in Germany, and its "bank," I am told, has never been broke.

The gaming is carried on at the *Kursaal*, the most remarkable building in the place, of vast dimensions. It is fitted up most magnificently, and is the centre of attraction in the town, containing, in addition to the gaming rooms, a great saloon for dancing, reading rooms, a splendid *restauration* and supper rooms. Attached to it are beautiful gardens, extensive enough to be called a park almost, with walks, fountains, lakes and terraces, all brilliantly illuminated in the evening. Here the visitors can sit in the open air and enjoy their ices and coffee, whilst a splendid band "discourses most excellent music." Admittance is entirely free, yet the most perfect order is preserved. The *restauration* is conducted upon the Parisian principle, and we found that a capital dinner could here be obtained at very moderate cost, everything, wine included, being of the finest quality and served at the lowest cost. All this, of course, is to make the *Kursaal* more attractive; but the liberality of the proprietors of the tables is by no means limited to that establishment. The town is beautified with fountains, statues and fine buildings, to all of which they have been the principal contributors. In fact, without its " hell " Weisbaden would be too dull a place for summer resort, even though its waters should be the best in the world.

Play goes on continually, from morning till night, beginning at noon, I believe, and ending at midnight. This season there are fewer visitors than ever before, on account of the war, but it appeared to me that the tables were full all the time. Not a loud word is spoken in the play-rooms: the everlasting wheel is whirling around, the cards are being constantly distributed, the players silently deposit their stakes upon their chosen color or number, but no noise is heard. I watched the play and the players. It is a fascinating excitement, and the chances of winning appear so fair that it requires strong principles to resist the desire to try "just once." When the rooms are crowded and play runs high, the excitement is feverish, but still quite silent. Many people pass most of their waking hours at the tables, I am told. At least one fourth of the players are women. I saw one very old, white-haired, toothless, almost palsied female, who, it was said, played regularly every day. She was sitting with little piles of gold and silver before her, and keeping notes of the result of every game. Now and then with trembling hand she placed her money on the board, apparently with the

greatest system, but whether she won or lost her face
gave no visible sign. Near her sat a man and his
wife — " both were young, and she was fair." They
also were regular players, and quite wealthy. She
kept notes whilst he made calculations. Next them
a man so thin, so sallow and gaunt, that he might
have served for an image of death. His face was an
anatomical study, so tightly drawn was every muscle.
He looked like a poor man, yet he played with gold
pieces entirely. But I must take you away from this
demoralizing spectacle.

At Wiesbaden the party of sixteen, who had been
together a month, broke up — some going one way,
some another. Our Buffalo friends were intending
to spend some weeks in the neighborhood of the
Baths, and I would have been glad to stay with them,
but my holiday was fast running away, and I was
mindful of a certain promise not to overstay it; and
there was Switzerland, France and England yet to be
visited, according to my plans. For these reasons I
broke away quite suddenly one evening and went to
Frankfort-on-the-Maine, about an hour's ride per rail
from Wiesbaden.

At Frankfort I noted very little to write about,
though the town is one of the most important of any
I have visited. Here is the original of the great
banking houses of the Rothschild family. A little
business took me to the institution two or three times,
and the thing I most admired about it was the per-

fect politeness with which every one was treated by the clerks. I was groping my way along the dark halls, looking at the inscriptions on the doors, trying to find the proper "bureau" for my business. A clerk came out with a handful of papers. "Can I have the pleasure of assisting you, sir?" said he with a polite bow. It seems to me that I remember two or three young bank clerks not far from Buffalo who might take a lesson from this incident. Immense as is the business of the house, the smallest customers are treated with as much apparent consideration as the most important.

The pride of Frankfort, in an artistic sense, is Donnaker's great statue of Ariadne, which is exhibited at a villa near one of the town gates. It is a truly beautiful work, so familiar to everybody from the pretty little statuettes of it to be seen at every shop where such things are sold, that a description of it would be superfluous. Its greatest peculiarity to me was the difficulty to decide, as it was turned slowly around on its revolving pedestal, from which point of view it was most to be admired. From Frankfort we made a carriage excursion to Homburg, about ten miles, another fashionable gambling and watering place, where the *Kursaal* is more magnificent still than at Weisbaden, and brings all the business there is done at the place. It is a town of hotels and lodging houses, and, like Weisbaden, has no other dependence for an existence than the visits of invalids and

gamblers. In case the Prussians obtain all these mi-
nor States in North Germany one good result will
surely grow out of it — viz: the closing of these le-
galized " hells."

A great deal of excitement was manifested at
Frankfort, which is the capital of the German Confederation, over the news of the tremendous defeat
of the Austrians under Marshal Benedek in Bohemia.
Here we heard that the Emperor Francis Joseph had
ceded Venetia to France, and that the latter power
had made a demand on Prussia to consent to an armistice. Poor Austria! If she could only have done
this in the beginning, the war, as well as her great
humiliation, might have been avoided. Francis Joseph says that the honor of the Austrian arms being
vindicated by the great victory in Venetia, he can
consent to negotiations. Fine words! — but how
different is the actual state of the case! The Prussians are very mad at Napoleon's intervention —
some of them so very mad as to declare that Victor
Emmanuel gave the victory to Austria in order to
bring about this action of the Emperor. What an
absurd notion!

From Frankfort we took the train to Heidelburg,
where we arrived at midnight, and here I stop this
letter.

VI.

HEIDELBERG, ITS TRADITIONS, ITS CASTLE AND ITS QUARREL-
SOME STUDENTS. — A POOR SCHOLAR. — STRASBURG, ITS
CATHEDRAL AND THE WONDERFUL CLOCK. — A BRIEF TRIP
IN SWITZERLAND, AND SOME BRIEFER NOTES ABOUT IT. —
THE ALPS.

GENEVA, SWITZERLAND, July 19, 1866.

The last has been a very busy week with me, and
I shall find it somewhat difficult to give you even a
dim idea of all we have seen in that brief period, in
one letter, though that should prove anything but
brief. My last letter took you with me to Heidelberg, I believe, where it rather abruptly closed, being
finished, as I had not time to tell you then, whilst a
carriage was waiting to take us to the railway station. Most of my writing is done in the midst of
hurry and bustle, or else when I ought to be in bed
and asleep: unfavorable circumstances which I pray
my readers to take into account.

Although we spent too little time in Heidelberg to
be able to give you anything like an adequate idea

of the beauties of the place, we made the most of what time we did have. We drove up the *König-stuhl* (King's stool), the highest hill in the vicinity, which almost deserves the more dignified name of mountain. On the summit is a lofty tower of one hundred and thirty-seven steps, from which we obtained a most charming view. Before us were spread the valleys of the Rhine and the Neckar, which latter river runs through the town. In the distance were the Haardt mountains and the ridge of the Black Forest. We were told that the spire of the Strasburg cathedral — ninety miles off — could be seen from this tower, but we certainly did not see it, though we had the aid of a pretty good glass, and it was a bright, clear day. The entire hill was covered with a luxuriant growth of trees, thousands upon thousands of chestnuts of enormous size being then in full blossom. On the way up the hill, we had stopped at the Wolf's Brunnen, a lovely little retired nook with a pretty spring which gives the place its name. It was here, according to tradition, that the great enchantress Jetta, who lived on the spot, was torn in pieces by a wolf. There was a cosy little tavern, and hard by were several ponds in which were vast quantities of trout of all sizes — the biggest by themselves. We saw them fed. In the third pond, great hungry monsters of five and six pounds weight came leaping out of the water when the bait was thrown. I think there must have been thousands of trout in this pond.

The house is famous for them and its beer. You order trout and beer. They catch the trout, and whilst the cooking is going on you sharpen your appetite with beer of delicious flavor, which is given to you in bottles taken out of a cave or cellar cut in the solid rock. I don't like beer — think it a stupid, heavy, and mawkish sort of drink, generally speaking — but I found a big glass of this cool, light beer was not too big.

On this same hill — or rather at the foot of it, but still considerably above the town — stands the famous castle of Heidelberg, one of the most imposing and interesting ruins in Europe. I presume all your readers have seen pictures of it. It has a history too long for this place. We spent some hours about the ruins and grounds, and would like to have spent days. Parts of the castle are still inhabited, and the grounds and gardens are kept in very good order. You have heard of the great Heidelberg tun, the largest wine cask in the world — thirty-six feet long and twenty-five feet high — holding eight hundred hogsheads, or considerably over a quarter of a million of bottles! It is in the cellars of this castle, and is one of the great sights of the place. I could hardly realize the immensity of its size until I had walked round it, from the bottom to the top, in the gallery which encircles it. But, alas! it has been empty for the last century!

Heidelberg has suffered from the horrors of war to a greater extent than almost any town in Europe, and yet it does not appear to love a quiet life yet. At least the students of its famous University are a very quarrelsome set. We saw a little inn where they fight their duels, and were told that four or five of these encounters sometimes take place in a single day, and that it is no uncommon thing for a student to have been engaged in twenty or thirty, as principal, in the course of four or five years. Fortunately fatal results do not often follow. It appeared to me that these duels were regarded as one of the institutions of the town. Almost everybody spoke of them, and pictures of such a contest were everywhere to be seen. At the shops where such things were sold, it was thought so much a matter of course that tourists must want one of these pictures as a memento of Heidelberg that I made a point of refusing, in my obstinate may, you know. There are about seven hundred students in the University, and they certainly appear to outnumber the rest of the inhabitants.

While we were exploring the castle, as I had almost forgotten to note, we observed a very fine-looking and well-dressed young man on the terrace, apparently admiring the beauties of the scene. He approached and surprised me with a request for assistance, saying he was on his travels and out of money. I was told that such incidents were of frequent occurrence. Scholars and students start off on a tour on foot and depend for their expenses upon the success of appeals of this kind, and no one thinks any shame is involved in the transaction, except, indeed, to any one who is able and refuses to assist them.

From Heidelberg we made an excursion to Strasburg, solely to see the great Cathedral, and I need hardly tell you that we felt well repaid for the visit. The spire of the Cathedral is the highest in the world, being nearly five hundred feet above the pavement. When I tell you that I panted my way up three hundred and twenty-eight steps on a mortal hot day, knowing my constitutional objection to labor of that sort, you will not be surprised to hear that I would not go any higher, though I was still only half way up to the pinnacle. I was glad to stop and rest, surveying the scene the while, which was hardly worth the exertion it had cost. Mostly the chimney tops and blackened roofs of Strasburg, with here and there a solitary stork standing on one leg, "monarch of all he surveyed," and looking as proud and complacent, perched up there, as though the house had been built specially to afford a good foundation for his nest. When I had recovered breath I could not sufficiently admire the singular beauty of the airy lace-work of stone, now more clearly to be seen, which is the conspicuous characteristic of the Cathedral tower. If the original design had been carried out, there would be two towers of equal height. Only one is complete: the other probably never will be. Modern art dreads to compete with those sturdy stone-workers of old, whose wonderfully original conceptions were so skillfully and daringly executed that one knows not which most to admire — the beauty of the design, the perfection of the workmanship, or the persever-ance and bravery which must have been displayed in overcoming the engineering difficulties involved in doing such massive work at such immense heights. Think of it! This perfect piece of architecture was designed six hundred years ago. How little progress has art made in that direction in all these centuries! If all other branches of human acquirements had stood as still where would the world be now? It is an in-teresting fact in the history of this Cathedral that the work was continued after the death of the architect, Erwin of Steinbach, by his son, and afterward by his daughter Sabina. She was a sculptor as well as an ar-chitect, and carved several statues for the interior which still remain to attest her skill. They are very quaint-looking pieces of work. A statue of Sabina herself stands in one of the porches. This whole fam-ily of architects were buried within the Cathedral.

The people of Strasburg have preserved such por-tions of the ornamental work of the Cathedral as have had to be restored on account of decay. We inspect-ed a very large number of interesting relics of this character in an ancient house near the Cathedral, said to have been erected in the eighth century. The great architect himself lived in this house, and it has an elegant Gothic winding staircase of stone, worked

from the master's own design.   Here is preserved the
wonderful old clock which, after remaining for some
centuries, became unable to perform its work.   It
was removed, and another, precisely like it in respect
to mechanical contrivances but much more perfect in
workmanship, has been constructed.   We were among
a curious crowd in the Cathedral, who gathered at
noon to see it strike.   As the hand pointed to the
hour a figure representing Childhood passes in front
of an image of Death and strikes the first quarter on
a bell; then follows Youth striking the second, Man-
hood the third, and Old Age the fourth.   Death
strikes the hour.   This much is done every hour; but
at noon, in addition to this, the figures of the twelve
Apostles are seen slowly passing in front of an image
of the Saviour, who blesses them as they bow before
him.   During this time a cock, twice life-size, flaps
his wings and crows three times, a wonderful imita-
tion of nature.   This extraordinary clock is about
twenty feet high, and is as beautiful in appearance as
it is wonderful in its working.   It has a perpetual
calendar with the movable feasts, an orrery after the
Copernican system showing the tropical revolutions
of the planets, the phases of the moon, the eclipses of
the sun and moon calculated forever, the true time
and the siderial time, and many other astronomical
particulars which I have not room to give.

We left Strasburg without tasting one of its famous
pies, and in about four hours were in Switzerland,

stopping first at Basle, one of the richest towns of
the Republic, situated on the Rhine at the junction
of the frontiers of Germany, France and Switzerland.
Here we tarried two days, more for the purpose of
rest than because there was anything particularly interesting about the place. The Rhine flowed beneath
our windows in a swifter current than I had elsewhere seen it, and we could look up and down the
stream a long distance, obtaining either way a charming view. At this place I find I made but very few
notes, and there was only one incident which secured
a place in my memory, but that I will give you.
First, however, you must know that I had begun to
pride myself not a little on the facility with which I
had been able to make myself understood by people
unacquainted with my speech, through a pretty free
use of my hands and other dumb language. Indeed,
I had achieved quite a reputation in our party as a
pantomimist, and was often appealed to when all
other means of communicating with the natives had
proved of no avail. Well, this self-conceit received a
heavy blow at Basle, from which it has never entirely
recovered. We were driving into the suburbs some
miles to visit Birseck Castle, a curious old ruin near
Arlesheim. The day was hot and the way was dusty.
We met a woman with a basket of fine juicy-looking
cherries, refreshing to look at. We wanted some. I
stopped the driver and explained to him by signs,
which I had begun to think infallible, that he should

call the woman back. "*Ja wohl!*" said he, nodding his head a dozen times, as much as to say he understood me perfectly. He got down, went back, and (I was already beginning to select money to pay for the cherries) — put up the top of the carriage! When he returned to his seat he looked so proud of having understood me so quickly that I had not the heart to undeceive him, especially as the woman and the cherries in the meantime were half a mile behind us. But I have not bragged so much about my "signs" working wonders since that incident.

From Basle to Berne was a four-hours' ride, through a beautiful and mountainous country which realized to us that we were in Switzerland at last. The railway has many tunnels: one, said to be the longest in the world, the train was nearly six minutes in running through. The route takes a very zigzag course all the way, but always with some charming landscape in view. It would require more space than you can spare me were I to attempt a description of this wonderfully beautiful country, even as seen from the railway, and I shall therefore condense into brief paragraphs many things about which I could with greater ease fill pages. Realize to yourself that in order to make my letters keep pace with my travels, I must, in the remainder of this epistle, tell of nearly a week in Switzerland, and then you will not wonder that I am so strongly inclined to abandon the task entirely.

I shall never forget my first impressions as a magnificent view of the entire chain of the Bernese Alps was spread before us when the train had nearly reached Berne. The day was beautifully clear, the sky blue and cloudless, and the outlines of the snow-capped mountains were so sharp and distinct that one found it difficult to realize that they were still nearly forty miles distant. But the snow did not look like snow. The glow of the sun was upon the face of the mountains, and I fancied they were of pure burnished silver, and that I saw them through a veil of gold. Or, perhaps, if I compare them to a pile of fleecy clouds tinged with the rays of the setting sun, you will have a clearer idea of the mountains as they first appeared to me.

The commanding views of the Alps and the snow-clad peaks of the Bernese Oberland which are to be had in clear weather from almost every open space in the city, form the great attraction of Berne to the tourist, though it is a very interesting town aside from this. It is the capital of the Swiss Republic, and the tourist who has the leisure may spend a week there very profitably, learning more, perhaps, of the peculiarities of the people and the characteristics of the government than at any other of its cities. I visited the National Council Chambers, and was much struck with the simple yet massive grandeur of the rooms. An animated debate was going on in the lower Chamber whilst I was there. The speakers use the German, French or Italian languages, as may

5

best suit them. The President's speeches, and motions and resolutions, when offered in German, are translated into Italian and French by an official interpreter.

A foreigner is certain to be astonished at the number of representations of bears which meet his eye at every prominent position. Bruin is the heraldic emblem of Berne, the symbol of the power of the city, and the citizens have placed statues of him, armed and equipped with sword, banner, helmet and shield, in the gardens, on the squares, at the corners of streets, and on fountains, pumps and gates. Half-a-dozen great monsters are kept in a public den at the public expense, and the people are prohibited by law from offering them anything that would be hurtful to their delicate stomachs. In fact there are bears, alive or in effigy, everywhere. The stranger will see children in the street devouring bread bears. He can never turn his head, indeed, without seeing some kind of an image of Bruin.

The streets of Berne are long and tolerably straight, and the houses are of immense strength, the ground floor fronts, especially in the older parts of the city, being open and arched, with little shops back, and stalls in the arches, so that the pedestrian can walk the whole length of many streets in a sort of arcade. This peculiarity of the buildings constitutes one of the quaintest features of the city. There are an immense number of fountains and pumps, and in the middle of many of the streets wide channels are cut through which rapid streams of clear water constantly flow.

We visited a public garden in the evening, where we obtained from the terrace a sublime view of the Alps at sunset. More than fifty mountains or peaks of mountains could be counted; the magnificent Jungfrau, the Monk and the Eiger, being the most prominent. We were fortunate enough to see the glow of the Alps which is so much spoken of in the Guide-Books. Long after the sun had set in the valleys, and indeed after its rays had disappeared from the loftiest peaks of the mountains, those snowy Alps were ruddy with a hovering glow, as though bright fires within shone through their cold faces.

At Berne there are swimming baths in the river Aare, which might be imitated on our own Niagara, with very little expense and with very great advantage to our citizens. The Aare is a cold and extremely rapid stream. On its banks are many bathing-houses, cheaply constructed, but affording excellent baths. When I see how many public institutions of this kind there are in every little town in Switzerland, where a river offers the opportunity, and notice how well they are patronized, I blush for Buffalonians, who make such scant use of the noble Niagara.

From Berne we made an excursion to Interlaken, and I wish I could take your readers with me, in imagination, at least — though, indeed, the *wish* is all there will be of it, for my pen cannot convey the faintest idea of the impressions made upon my memory in this delightful trip. First is a railway journey of about an hour, at every minute of which the tourist wishes he could stop and enjoy the prospect. This brings him to the Lake of Thun, a "deeply, darkly, beautifully blue" sheet of water, about twelve miles long and three wide, the greater portion of its banks studded with picturesque villas and gardens, or else steep and precipitous hills, which would be mountains in any other country. A pretty little steamer took us the length of this lake. Ever-changing views of the still distant Alps were presented, and when the boat stopped we could hardly believe that an hour and a half had passed away in the trip.

The steamer stops at Neuhaus, a village about two miles from Interlaken, but a crowd of carriages and omnibusses are always in readiness to convey the passengers to the hotels at the latter place. On the way we pass through Unterseen, a very old town, which has been quite left in the background owing to the attractions offered by Interlaken, its more fashionable neighbor. We stopped at the Hotel Victoria, a new and exceedingly handsome house, where we had rooms with the glorious Jungfrau in full view at every window. What shall I say of this majestic mountain? We spent three days in its neighborhood, where we could see it in different aspects nearly all the time, but I am dumb when I would express my

admiration. Perhaps I had better content myself
with this silent tribute, for the space to which I limit
each letter is now nearly exhausted, and Interlaken is
still left "undone." Indeed I am tempted not to take
you with me any further this post; but, alas! I am
further advanced on my journey, and shall be still
more "cabined, cribbed, confined" in my next, if I do
not bring my account down to date in this.

More strangers congregate during the summer at
Interlaken than at any other point in Switzerland,
and I presume it is, at the same time, as really fashionable a resort as it is popular. The place itself has
hardly a thousand inhabitants, but it has nearly a
dozen first-class hotels, and twice as many respectable
"pensions," boarding houses, and smaller hotels.
The larger houses are of magnificent dimensions, and
are as elegantly furnished and served as the best hotels in New York. In fact the Victoria reminded me
more of a popular New York hotel than any other
I have yet stopped at in Europe. The best of the
houses are built fronting the Jungfrau, a fact which
none of their proprietors forget to mention in their
advertisements, and I have heard it whispered that it
is sometimes put down in the bills. There is no place
in Switzerland from which so many delightful excursions can be conveniently made, and it is for this
reason perhaps that so many travelers make Interlaken their headquarters; and this latter fact, again,
accounts for the greater degree of dress and fash-

ion which is here to be seen than elsewhere. Interlaken is the Saratoga of Switzerland, and I would
advise lady tourists to take their best clothes there,
if they must carry their big trunks anywhere in
that country.

My time was so limited that I could only make two
of the excursions from Interlaken, out of the many
which have been so often and so enthusiastically described. The first was by carriage to Lauterbrunnen,
a place which takes its name (meaning "nothing but
brooks") from the numerous brooks and springs
which rise in the lofty rocks of the neighborhood.
At least a score of these miniature Niagaras leap
from the immense heights hereabouts. The most famous of them — the Staubbach — has an unbroken fall
of nearly a thousand feet, and its waters are so spread
and separated before they reach the bottom that they
become a transparent sheet of spray and mist, which
is waved and twisted by the breeze into fantastic and
graceful forms, upon which the rays of the mid-day
sun, as we saw it, wrought a succession of beautiful
rainbows constantly rising and descending. I put my
foot in one of these rainbows, and got wet through
for my pains by the almost impalpable shower which
fell upon me from the tiny cataract above. From
this place we returned a little way and branched off
to Grindenwald, by a steep ascending road for several
miles. On the way by this winding path we saw the
majestic Jungfrau from many different points of view.

We had seen the sun rise upon its vast and dazzling peaks at Interlaken long before we started, and the previous evening had wondered at its beauty when it was blushing in the lingering embrace of the ardent god of day — fleecy clouds veiling its face at times, and then lifting their folds again, as if at the will of a coy and modest, yet somewhat coquetish damsel — but we thought the closer view we had at mid-day showed the glorious mountain in its most imposing and beautiful aspect.

There are great glaciers at Grindenwald, descending so far into the valley as to be easy of access. One of these we visited, passing on the narrow foot-path thither scores of men and women wheeling big blocks of ice cut from the glaciers, destined for the Paris market. Huge natural caverns are formed in this great ice mountain, and we walked into an artificial one which was cut into the solid ice a distance of perhaps forty feet. Two men were at work there, cutting another arch at a right angle. In the corner a woman was playing some unfamiliar instrument and singing a still more unfamiliar air. The noise was awful. Great drops of sweat kept falling from the ice, and I had a fellow feeling for it. I don't think I should have appreciated the music any better if I had been acquainted with the sentiment; but you need not fancy that I was a "dead-head" at that entertainment.

This glacier is at the foot of Mount Eiger, which is

twelve thousand two hundred and forty feet high,
and the whole valley is here shut in by monster peaks
covered with eternal snow.   The ice cut from the
glacier is beautifully clear, but mottled as though it
was formed in layers and ridges, like a great icicle.
I should not be willing to forgive myself had I missed
the visit to the spot, though we were very tired
when we returned to Interlaken, for the day had
been an extremely hot one.   Our way going and
coming was beset with beggars and half-beggars, the
latter offering some equivalent in the shape of toys
or fruits or milk for the money they demanded.   I
notice that the Guide-Books speak of this as the most
disagreeable feature of travel in Switzerland, but I
think they make too much of it.   The poor people are
satisfied with so small a gratuity that a dollar scattered judiciously will strew blessings on the tourist's
path a whole day's journey, even where beggars most
abound.   The Alpine horn is particularly execrated,
but the fellow who blew the lusty blast for me, waking the echoes from the surrounding mountains, furnished me a pleasure for which I was quite willing to
pay the customary trifle.   Our musical critic would
have found melody in the echoes, I know, though he
might have stopped his ears, perhaps, at the original
notes.

Our next excursion was to the Geissbach, where
we spent a night.   We went by a small steamer on
the beautiful little lake of Brienz, less than eight miles

long and only about two miles broad, but with water at some places two thousand feet deep. It is not a difficult ascent from the landing to a pleasant spot on this mountain, where a snug hotel is to be found. Here were excellent accommodations, and a great many visitors. The view from the terrace of the hotel is the most charming one which my eyes have ever looked upon. Below is the lake enclosed by mountains; above is the Geissbach with its seven cascades which precipitate themselves from rock to rock, the highest more than a thousand feet above the lake; all around are great trees, and vines, and flowers, and hills covered with a most exquisite verdure. Behind several of the cascades are little bridges on which we stood next morning and viewed the landscape through the falling waters, having risen very early and climbed what was to us a great height for the purpose. I wish I could convey to you an idea of how the cascades appeared the night before when they were illuminated by floods of blue and crimson and green lights, but I can only leave it to your imagination.

This early exploration, a visit to Brienz, return to Interlaken, and from thence to Berne, made a pretty hard day's work, and we were glad to rest at the latter place for the night. Next day we started for Geneva, where we arrived yesterday, after a delightful trip, of which I shall give you no description in this, having taken up more than my usual space already.

5*

The first person we met as we walked into the hotel, was young Mr. J. P. W., and very glad indeed were we to see him, for it was now more than two weeks since we had seen a face from home. This evening Dr. and Mrs. W., and Miss D., arrived in a carriage from Mont Blanc. These unexpected meetings with friends so far away from home, and the opportunities they give to compare notes and news, are the pleasantest incidents which the tourist has to record.

We leave to-morrow for Paris, and if I write you again it will be from that gay metropolis.

VII.

THE ROUTE FROM BERNE TO GENEVA. — THE LAKE OF GENE-
VA. — SOME NOTES ABOUT THE SWISS METROPOLIS. —
FIRST ENCOUNTER WITH FRENCH, AND PERPLEXITY
THEREAT. — ARRIVAL AT PARIS. — A WEEK OF SIGHT-SEE-
ING IN THE GAY CITY. — SPECULATIONS ABOUT THE GER-
MAN DIFFICULTY. — THE ATLANTIC CABLE.

PARIS, July 29, 1866.

I think there was a promise in my last letter to
give you some particulars about Geneva in the first
that I should write you from Paris, as I had neither
room nor time just then. I am sorry now that I did not
make the room and steal the time, though that letter
was already too long, for I find that a very few days
in this bewildering metropolis are sufficient to make
the impressions of immediately preceding events appear very dim indeed. So much have I seen in my
short sojourn here that it seems a ridiculous thing to
think of writing about any previous matters; yet,
more for the sake of preserving the unities in these
hurried records of a too-brief European trip than be-

cause your readers would care about it if I did not, I
will endeavor to keep my promise.   One word of advice first, however, to such chance readers as may
contemplate a visit to Europe, and rashly intend to
write letters thereupon, viz: don't think of writing
anything but *Paris* when *in* Paris; or, better still,
don't think of writing at all!

The trip from Berne to Geneva took us through a
very interesting country, of which we saw all too little from the windows of the railway carriage.   Fortunately, however, we only proceeded as far as Lausanne by rail — a journey of about four hours, passing through the old town of Freiburg, where travelers with more leisure should be sure to stop, if only
to see the beautiful Cathedral, and to hear its great
organ, considered one of the finest in Europe, with
sixty-seven stops and seven thousand eight hundred
pipes, some of them thirty-two feet in length.   At
Lausanne, also, where we had only two or three hours,
more days could have been profitably and pleasantly spent.   If I had not determined to write about
such things only as I have seen, I could fill this letter
with sketches of delightful excursions which can be
made from this place.   Is it not aggravating to think
that we were only a few hours from Vevay, from
Montreux, and the Castle of Chillon — in the neighborhood where Byron resided so long — and could
not spare those few hours?   After all, I fear there
will be as many regrets as pleasant reminiscences con-

nected with my visit to Europe, for, when it is over, I shall be constantly forgetting what I have seen, and thinking of what I did not see.

It seems to me that the first view of the Lake of Geneva — which is suddenly disclosed to the traveler just as he emerges from a long dark tunnel, a few minutes before reaching Lausanne — is one of such singular beauty that it would be thought a sufficient recompense for a long day's journey. It struck me so forcibly that I involuntarily cried "stop!" as I had so frequently done in our carriage rides lately, quite forgetting that the iron horse was entirely beyond my control. In one direction lay the valley of the Rhone, backed in the distance by the mountains of Savoy; in the foreground numerous villages nestled in the midst of vineyards; in the centre of the picture, the deep blue beautiful Lake surrounded by mountains. Words — certainly my words — are totally inadequate to convey an idea of this charming scene.

At Lausanne we took a steamer which conveyed us down the Lake in about four hours to Geneva. Do not expect any description of this sail. I was too much occupied to make notes, and if I attempted to say anything about my impressions now it would be like the delighted but incoherent talk of a child who has just for the first time seen a panorama. Yet there was one disappointment about it, too, for we had been taught to expect a view of Mont Blanc

from one point; but either the atmosphere was not
clear enough (yet it was a fine day), or our eyes were
not good (mine are generally quite useful, though not
considered ornamental) — at any rate Mont Blanc
was not visible to us.   There was compensation,
though, in the view of Geneva from the Lake.   Of all
the cities we have visited I think this is the most
charmingly situated.   The "arrowy Rhone" shoots
out of the Lake and divides the town.   Magnificent
broad bridges span the rapid stream.   At night a
myriad of gas lamps are lit along these bridges, as
though intended for an illumination.   Reflected in
the clear stream these lights have such a peculiarly
brilliant effect that one hardly realizes the scene to
be one of everyday life.   Between two of the finest
bridges there is a little island, named after the great
sophist, J. J. Rousseau, who was a native of the town.
A small suspension bridge connects this island with
one of the great bridges, and on it is a statue of Rousseau, in the midst of a pretty garden.   The island,
indeed, is all garden and promenade.   Coming into
Geneva from the Lake all this is seen at once.   Both
banks of the Rhone have broad, substantial quays
and handsome buildings, and the shores of the Lake,
before it runs into the Rhone, are thickly dotted with
beautiful villas and grounds.   On the Grand Quay,
where the steamers stop, there is a fine public promenade called the English Garden, very neatly laid out,
and a favorite resort with the people.   This has appa-

rently been stolen from the Lake, as its walls run into the water in the form of a broad wedge.

Geneva has at least a dozen hotels which would rank as first-class at any Metropolis in the world. Some of these are very large and imposing buildings, and all are seen from the Lake, apparently bidding the traveler welcome. I don't know how many smaller hotels there are, but I should think that nearly half the city is made up of public houses of one sort or other. The town is said to have less than fifty thousand inhabitants, but it certainly is the biggest town of that size I ever saw. I presume the transient population must be nearly as large as the resident, for Geneva is as pleasant a place to stop at as there is anywhere. Apart from its natural advantages, however, and its celebrated schools, I believe it has not a great many attractions to boast of, except in the way of fine shops, of which it has a vast number. It's a very nice place to " go shopping " in, I assure you. In this respect Geneva is a miniature Paris, and travelers who happen to stop there before going to the latter place may advantageously dispose of some of their shopping money, for they will find Paris styles at much less than Paris prices. This is especially true of jewelry and fancy articles. Watches are its speciality, and there are many great manufactories at this place famous all over the world. I was politely conducted through the largest — that of the celebrated house of Messrs. Patck, Phillippe & Co.

—and what I saw there of the mysteries of horology will forever remain a wonder to me.

I need not tell you that Geneva has been the home of many famous people. John Calvin lived here thirty years. Necker, the minister of Louis XVI., and his daughter, Madame de Staël, were born here. Voltaire had a chateau in the neighborhood, and it is still one of the sights which the traveler is expected to visit. But I think the Genevese are prouder of Jean Jacques Rousseau than of any of their other celebrities. Many of the shops use his name for a sign. I noticed a great tailor shop with " *à* J. J. Rousseau," in huge gilt letters over the door, and, directly opposite, an establishment for ladies' under-garments, having the same distinguished title. Any one will show you the house where the "wild self-torturing sophist" was born; or the houses, I might say, for there are two for which the honor is claimed. Not being an admirer of Rousseau, myself, these spots possessed so little attraction for me that I was ready to exclaim, " a plague o' both your houses! "

Geneva is essentially a French town, although the metropolis of Switzerland. It abounds in *cafés* whose customers take their ease and their ices on the sidewalks, under little awnings, in the true Parisian fashion. In other parts of the miniature Republic we found German the native tongue, though French was generally understood; but in Geneva the latter language was the only one in common use. I had hardly been prepared for this, and was quite upset when I found that the little German which had been picked up by a very young gentleman of our party, who had been at school in Dresden, was no longer of any use to us. I may as well confess that I had looked forward with something of dread to our anticipated visit to Paris. Indeed, I didn't want to go to France until I knew the lingo, for if I did, I knew, like Hood, I would repent, by jingo! — but I had not expected that our lack of French would be felt before we arrived in that country. Knowing what a horror I have of asking questions of strangers, even in my own country, you will readily imagine how disgusted I was to find myself suddenly obliged to ask a great many, and nine times out of ten to receive only a shake of the head, a smile, or a shrug, in reply. You will not be surprised, therefore, to learn that I was not in the most amiable temper the first few hours of our stay in Geneva; but you would be amused if you could realize how irritable and porcupinish I was at being roused out of a troubled sleep, at a very early hour the first morning (it was market day and my room fronted on the market place), by a lot of poultry-women jabbering and wrangling under my window in the fastest, most aggravatingly unintelligible French it was possible to string together. It seemed to me that the very cocks, about which the women appeared to be quarreling, crowed in French, and crowed through their noses, too, the nastiest, meanest little crows you ever heard! It quite spoilt my appetite for breakfast.

After a little while, though, I found that it was only a bugbear which had frightened me, and that patience and good-humor carried us along nicely. The people are polite and attentive; they try their best to understand a foreigner, and, if the foreigner keeps his temper, they generally succeed. In most of the shop windows are little signs, "English spoken," and at all the hotels there are sure to be hosts or waiters to whom the traveler who has no other language can make known his wants. I stayed at Geneva long enough to learn these facts, and left that town a wiser and a better-tempered man than I entered it. Fourteen hours by rail brought us to Paris, where we have now been just a week, stopping at the *Hotel du Rhin*, in the Place Vendôme, with the great Vendôme Column, erected by Napoleon to commemorate his victories over the Austrians and Russians in 1805, right in front of our window. In this hotel the present Emperor resided in 1848, when he was a deputy to the National Assembly. I hope the fact will be forgotten when my bill is made out!

A week in Paris, and a *first* week in Paris, too! Think of it! Try and form an idea of how much a not idle man, enjoying good health and bent upon sight-seeing, must have done in that length of time, and then expect me to "write it up" in half a letter if you can! I shall not attempt to do it. The most

I shall essay to give will be a rapid sketch — merely a list only — of the places I have visited, and leave my readers to their memories, or to their libraries, for further particulars. I may say beforehand, however, that I could not have done half as much in double the time without the assistance of a faithful and competent interpreter and guide who had been recommended to me by some friends I met in Germany. I advise all strangers in Paris to procure the services of such a person, for the first week or two at any rate. They can be had at any good hotel, and their fees are so moderate (six francs a day) that the money is more than saved in hack hire, admission fees, gratuities, etc., for which the stranger generally over-pays, unless he has the advice of some one *au fait* in such matters.

My first day in Paris was one of rest. I found letters and papers waiting my arrival, and to answer the first and read the last kept me pleasantly occupied whilst getting rested. Was I not glad to find so many impressions of your broad, clean, nice-looking face, you dear old *Commercial?* One must go abroad to properly appreciate his daily newspaper. Letters — long letters too — are still more welcome. I wish some of my friends had not forgotten this fact. But this is not "doing" Paris. I begun my acquaintance with the gay metropolis by walking and driving about the streets pretty nearly the whole of one day — a plan I would recommend to all visitors, as one gets a

general idea of the city in that way, and a sort of fa-
miliarity with its aspect, which are very serviceable.
We commenced sight-seeing by a visit to the Tomb
of Napoleon, that grand monument of a nation's love,
to give an intelligible description of which would occupy more space than you could afford me for an
entire letter. The cover of the sarcophagus alone
weighs upward of sixty tons. It is a ponderous block
of reddish brown granite and was brought from Lake
Onega, in Finland, at a cost for transportation alone
of over thirty thousand dollars. This is exquisitely
polished, and looks like the dark stones we sometimes
see set in jewelry. The marble for this monument
cost nearly half a million of dollars, and more than
two millions of dollars have altogether been expended
on it. After this, during the day, we visited the Pan-
theon, the Church of St. Etienne du Mont, the Cathedral of Notre Dame, the Palace of Justice and the
Sainte Chapelle — the latter considered the most perfect Gothic edifice in Paris, a beautiful chapel which
has recently been restored at a cost of more than a
million of francs. The merest dryest details of what
we thus saw in one day would occupy many of your
columns; how then can I hope to convey even the
faintest idea of these things in the space at my command? I will not try. You must be satisfied to
know, in brief, that since that day we have visited
the Gallery of the Louvre twice, had a drive in the
Bois de Boulogne, attended a promenade concert in

the Champs Elysées, inspected the Pompeiien Palace
built by Prince Napoleon in the style of the house of
Diomedes at Pompeii, since sold to a speculator and
now exhibited to the curious public at a franc a head
— drove and walked about the beautiful little Parc
de Monceaux — spent an entire day at Versailles
(wish I could write you a whole letter about that) —
examined the great collection of Roman and Mediæval antiquities at the Hôtel de Cluny, where there
are immense stone baths still existing which were
used in the fourth century — and twice visited the
Luxembourg Palace with its great gallery of modern
paintings, and were conducted, also, at our last visit,
through the magnificent Senate Chamber, the Throne
Hall, the Consultation Room, the Chapel, and the
sleeping apartment of Marie de Médicis. Interspersed
with all this sight-seeing have been many walks in the
Boulevards and other fine streets, visits to theatres,
some shopping and much staring in the shop windows.
What you have heard and read of these places will
assure you that our first week in Paris has not been
an idle one, though I say so little about it.

But more interesting than any of the sights do I
find the people of Paris. "Paris is France," they
say, therefore I suppose one may fairly judge the people of the whole nation by the denizens of the city.
Outwardly nothing could present a more favorable
idea of happiness, peace and tranquility in a great nation, than does the capital city of France. Every-

where the appearance of thrift and prosperity strikes the careful observer. There is less squalid poverty, less begging, less apparent misery to be found in a week in the streets of Paris than can be seen without much search any day in New York. This may be owing to the strictness and efficiency of the police arrangements, yet I have never seen any attempt on the part of the police to interfere with the people. All is fair on the surface, and I find it hard to believe that beneath this calm exterior there slumbers the volcano which many profess to think is ready to burst forth at any moment and overthrow the present order of things. If there is a throne in Europe which looks secure to-day it is that occupied by Louis Napoleon. Thoroughly as I dislike and distrust his character, I cannot help admitting to myself that the material prosperity of France has been further advanced under his rule than at any other period in the history of the nation. Judged by results, he has won greater glory in this respect, than the founder of his line, and has proved himself to be truly "a ruler of men" — at least of *French* men. He has given them a new Paris, too, for the old city is being rapidly torn down, and its narrow, crooked, unwholesome streets and unsightly buildings replaced with broad, straight, handsome avenues and palatial edifices. The Paris of to-day would hardly be recognized, it is said, by a Parisian who had not seen it in ten years; and the improvements are being carried forward as vigorously as ever, so that one may safely predict that it will be the finest city the world ever saw if the present system is maintained a score of years longer. I do not know that these wholesale improvements are entirely satisfactory to the people. The effect has been to increase the cost of living enormously — rents, in particular, being so high in the new streets that the old residents have to keep going back further and further from the heart of the city they love. Old Parisians grumble about this. They can't afford to live in the new Paris, they say. Prophets are not wanting who predict that trouble will come of this yet.

The people, as I said before, look happy and contented, and I have realized, what I had so often heard before, that the French are the politest of all the wanderers from Babel. If you speak to a waiter you must address him as " Monsieur," or be guilty of an unpardonable want of courtesy; your *femme de chambre* is " Mademoiselle," and even the old woman who shows you a seat in the theatre must be called " Madame." All officials are models of civility, and I have not forgotten how pleased I was at the politeness of the customs officers when I was waiting to have my baggage inspected in the railway station. I had rather dreaded this ordeal. The passengers were all conducted into a waiting room, with their handbaggage, whilst their trunks and boxes were arranged on long benches in an adjacent room. Presently an official said to me in excellent English (how did he guess it was my mother tongue?) "please take all your baggage into that room," pointing to where the checked pieces were. It was all over in a few minutes. Only one trunk was unlocked, and the merest glance given to its contents — nothing was pulled about — and I was ready to drive to a hotel almost as quick as I would have been in America, in a city where no such form is gone through with.

A pleasant feature of this city is that hardly any fees are exacted at the public institutions; at few places are any even expected, Paris being very different from the cities of Germany in this respect, as I know, and England, too, as I am told. At all *cafés* and restaurants, however, the waiters expect a few cents gratuity when the bill is paid.

Here, by the way, I ought to branch off and write a chapter on the subject of *Cafés*, if I would pretend to give you an idea of street life in Paris. They are passed at almost every step, and those upon the principal streets are fitted up with great splendor and more or less taste. Frequented as they are by all Paris — brilliantly lighted at night, with chairs and small tables placed outside upon the pavements, at which both sexes set and discuss tea, coffee, chocolate, ices or liquors — the scene, to the promenader threading his way through the crowd, is one of peculiar animation and gaiety. The foreigner is amused to observe the perfect nonchalance with which the eating, drinking and flirting is thus carried on upon the open streets. No feature of Parisian life is more characteristic or striking to the stranger.

I should end this letter here, but it occurs to me that I ought to speak of the great events which are just now occurring, if only to assure you that the sights of Paris have not entirely crowded out of mind all other considerations. The armistice which is now in operation between allied Prussia and Italy and poor hard-driven Austria, has brought the chief interest in the tremendous struggle to Paris, Napoleon being the great umpire between the belligerents. The latest intelligence would seem to indicate that the war is at an end. You have not failed to notice what a narrow escape I had from being an eye-witness of the occupation of Frankfort by the Prussians. I had left that city only a day or two when they arrived, and from what I have lately read about the extreme severity they meted out to the Frankforters, there must have been trying times in the old Federal capital. You know that Bismarck ordered his generals to levy a contribution of seventy-five millions francs on the city, being at the rate of nearly two hundred dollars per head for every man, woman and child of its inhabitants. The citizens refused to pay, and General de Manteuffel threatened to bombard and pillage the city if they did not.

A gentleman lately arrived from Frankfort says that when General de Manteuffel, speaking to a deputation who complained of the contribution, let fall

6

the word "pillage," one of the members of the dele-
gation, Doctor Mylius, advanced and said : "General,
you utter a menace that you cannot carry out."
"How," exclaimed the General, "I cannot!   Learn
that I can, if I wish it, have your head rolling at my
feet."   "I know that very well," replied Doctor Mylius, "but as to pillaging Frankfort, you cannot do
that, for you do not command a horde of barbarians,
but a civilized army, who would not pillage even if
you commanded it."   General de Manteuffel, white
with rage, could not find a word to answer.   So the
newspapers say.

It appears that Bismarck was resolved to punish
Frankfort severely for the determined opposition to
his policy which its prominent men have always exhibited.   But I don't think the threat to pillage the
city will be carried out, even if the money is not paid,
for there is a universal outcry from the newspapers
of all Europe against such a course.   The news
now is that the demand will not be enforced.   There
is another anecdote in circulation, to the effect that
the great banker, Rothschild, of Frankfort, threatened
to break all the banks of Prussia if General de Manteuffel attempted to put his threat into execution.   It .
is astonishing to what a splendid success the audacity
of Bismarck has carried him.   He is to-day the fore-
most man in Europe, and his superb arrogance chal-
lenges admiration — at least from those who do not
have to submit to it.

In all these exciting events on the continent, you cannot but have observed how poor a part has been played by England — how utterly disregarded have been her wishes and her remonstrances. It seems to me that the proud people of that country must have felt deeply humiliated by the spectacle of England's impotence under the "peace at any price" policy which has been chosen by her rulers. In these fighting times a nation must be able — and *willing* too — to follow up its arguments with blows, if it would have its wishes heeded.

Yet there is some glory, too, just now, to compensate England for the mortification she has suffered in the loss of her European prestige. The news has been received of the successful laying of the Atlantic Cable, and the importance of that magnificent achievement is acknowledged by all the world. If it be true that "Peace hath her victories not less renowned than War," then this is a triumph of which England has reason to be as proud as Prussia is over the bloody glory she has won in that wonderful campaign which is just ended. The Paris journals loudly applaud England for the perseverance she has exhibited in the undertaking. The *Temps* thus expresses itself:

" If anything can console pacific and laborious democratic and liberal Europe for the cruel anguish it has for some time past been suffering — for the invasion of liberty and right, the progress of military rule, and the triumph of egotistical ambition and brute force, it is the great event which is to-day announced by a despatch from London. The laying down of

the Atlantic cable has succeeded; the *Great Eastern*, a vessel
which will for the future have a name in history, has fulfilled
its mission to the end; electrical communication is established
between the Old and the New Worlds.   Now is successfully
accomplished that memorable event, more fruitful in consequences than the sanguinary struggles by which Germany has
just been desolated; now has been gained that great victory
of human intelligence and science over the blind forces of Nature.   Henceforth, if the ocean remains clement and respects
the mysterious line laid in its depths, we shall live with the
same life as the people of the New Continent; henceforth we
shall feel immediately the pulsations of that great nation
which has established self-government on the other side of
the Atlantic, and realized the idea of Democracy in action.
To the tenacity of the English is due that great result; it is
English capital which for the third time has shown confidence
in the accomplishment of that great work.   Honor therefore
to Anglo-Saxon perseverance."

And the *Liberté* is still more enthusiastic, as you
will see from the following extract:

"This is truly a glorious victory!   This is the conquest
that we love, not obtained by man over man, but by man over
things!   To abridge distance, to suppress it!   To put seas
separated by isthmuses in communication!   To pass under
mountains which ice and snow cover during eight months
of the year!   To multiply bridges over rivers and mighty
streams!   To open on all coasts ports of refuge against mari-
time catastrophies!   To let all sovereigns correspond between
each other without any intermediary, save their most intimate secretary!   What great deeds of political worth might
be achieved if governments would seek in reason and in
science that which they have too long endeavored to effect
by violence and war!"

I shall try and write you one more letter before
leaving Paris.   Good-bye.

VIII.

PARIS, August 6th, 1866.

A man need not go away from home, you will very justly say, to write about the weather, and especially is it unnecessary if the man happens to be a citizen of breezy Buffalo, where there is as much weather, and as many different varieties in a given length of time as can be seen in any place in the world. I believe it also forms a staple topic of conversation in society there to quite as great an extent as anywhere, and, if my memory is not at fault, it is sometimes mentioned in the newspapers — occasionally, if not oftener, in your own columns, I have been told. But, in spite of all this, I must drag the time-honored and somewhat threadbare subject into this letter, for it has been quite as remarkable as any other fact which has

come under my observation. I had expected to suffer
from the heat very severely during my stay here, and,
indeed, the dread of that suffering was even greater
with me than the trouble I should experience through
ignorance of the "lingo." I believe it was noted in
my last letter how little real difficulty I had encountered in the latter respect, and now I have to record
that the former dread has proved equally a bugbear,
for nothing could be more charming than the weather
has been in Paris during the two weeks of my sojourn.
It has been mild, bright (but not too bright), and
balmy all the time. There has been no day on which
a moderately thick coat could not be worn with comfort; and you, who have so often seen me at this season of the year, mopping the streaming perspiration
from my face after a toilsome ascent to your sanctum,
will readily appreciate the grateful feelings which
move me to disregard all chances of being charged
with stupidity, and boldly commence a letter from
Paris with a paragraph on the weather. I am told
that it was blazingly hot in this city for several weeks
just previous to my arrival; but, thanks to my lucky
star (which evidently is not the dog star), "charming"
is the proper adjective for me to use. It has rained
two or three mornings, but, with a single exception,
has cleared off in time to permit us to go sight-seeing
as early as has been convenient.

Under these favorable circumstances you will infer
that we have done a good deal in that way since my

last letter was finished, and you would be justified in expecting something more interesting than weather items in this; but, alas, there is such a thing as having too many good subjects for descriptive writing, and one sometimes feels inclined to lay down the pen in despair, not knowing where to begin. At least I do, on this occasion. A good plan (though I have not always pursued it) is to take up matters in the order they occur — certainly I will try it this time.

I think we spent the next day after what was mentioned in my last, at Fontainebleau, but as I do not keep copies or even notes of what I send you, I cannot be positive. (Should I now and then " double " a topic you must excuse it on that ground.) I suppose some of my readers, bearing in mind the associations connected with Fontainebleau, will be shocked when I tell them that the visitor to Paris, whose time like mine is limited to sixteen days, had better omit this excursion, as he can spend the day it takes to better advantage in the city: but I cannot help it if they are, for that is my deliberate opinion. Not that there is any reason to feel disappointed at what one has seen, but because in the same time and with much less expense so much more might have been seen in Paris. This remark, mind you, applies only to those who purpose so brief a stay as I do: those who have plenty of time should by all means give a day to Fontainebleau, where they will certainly find much to interest and some things to surprise them.

It takes two hours by rail from Paris to reach Fontainebleau. There is nothing to note except the Palace, the Garden and the Forest. The town itself is very dull and quiet, having only about ten thousand inhabitants. It has broad clean streets, and one very handsome avenue nearly a mile long, where splendid lofty trees on both sides intertwine their branches at a great height, producing a magnificent natural aisle with an effect far beyond the art of Man, except when he avails himself of the aid of Nature, as in this case. There are several fine hotels in the town, their chief business, of course, being derived through excursion parties from Paris. Many elegant private residences, too, and some very stately ones, has Fontainebleau, it being a nice, slow, aristocratic place, where great people can live in grand style at much less expense than they can in the metropolis.

The palace has such an unprepossessing exterior that we were the more surprised and delighted at the magnificence which characterizes its interior. It was a favorite residence of the great Napoleon, and of course the present Emperor would not be so much like his uncle if he did not also like to live there. We entered by the court yard, where Napoleon parted from his Old Guard and Grenadiers after his abdication in 1814, and where he reviewed them again, not quite a year later, when he returned from Elba. We ascended the great staircase, shaped something like a horse shoe, whose crooked steps would have a strange

tale to tell, could they speak, of the thoughts which
must have choked the fallen conqueror when he de-
scended them, as he supposed, for the last time. We
were shown the room in which he signed his abdication, and the table — an ordinary little table of ma-
hogany — on which it was done; and went through
the adjacent bed-room where he slept, everything
being still preserved in the same order as when he
occupied it. Old as the palace is, its most interesting associations are connected with the present dynasty. Here the divorce of Napoleon from Josephine
took place. I fancied that the attendant, who had
been describing the apartments to us in a loud, grating, machine-like voice, spoke in a softer tone when
he mentioned that incident. It was in this palace
that Napoleon confined, during twenty-four days, the
dethroned King Charles IV. of Spain. Here, also, he
kept Pope Pius VII. prisoner a year and a half, in the
sumptuous apartments once occupied by Catherine de
Médicis, mother of three kings, and Anne of Austria,
mother of Louis XIV. We were shown the private
apartments and the grand reception rooms of the
present Imperial family, but you will not expect a description of them when I tell you that the limits of
this letter would be too circumscribed for that purpose. If I mention that we walked through the library of the Emperor and were shown the desk at
which he worked on his life of Julius Cæsar; — that
we were ("as a special favor") shown the private

6*

apartments of the Prince Imperial, where he sleeps in
much the same state as any other little boy whose
parents are tolerably well-to-do in the world; — that
we examined the famous Gobelins tapestry, looking
like paintings, and of priceless value; — that we stood
in the Chapel of St. Saturnin, which was consecrated
by Thomas à Beckett, in 1169, when he was absent
from England on account of his quarrel with Henry
II., the chapel having been since then several times
restored, last by Louis Philippe whose talented
daughter, the late Princess Mary, designed the subjects for the stained glass; — that we passed through
the four rooms which were occupied by Madame de
Maintenon and are still furnished as then, in one of
which Louis XIV. signed the revocation of the Edict
of Nantes; — if I merely mention these things, I repeat, you must try and be satisfied, though I say not
a word about a hundred other objects of interest we
saw in the palace.

We spent far the greater part of the day, however,
in walking about the Gardens and in drives through
the Great Forest. So beautiful are the grounds, and
so quiet and retired, we do not wonder that tired
royalty finds this a pleasanter residence than crowded
bustling Paris. The space occupied by the gardens
is immense. They are laid out in the English style,
and pretty sheets of water, fountains, statues, trim-
cut groves, and flowers of every clime, fill up the
scene. One of the largest ponds is filled with carp,

many of them of great size and venerable with extreme age. Near by is a little stall at which an old woman sells bread. Visitors amuse themselves by throwing in hard loaves, and seeing the fish in immense numbers tumble and push them about till they are softened by the water, when some half-dozen great hungry monsters generally come to the spot, disperse the crowd, and devour the spoils. The Forest is sixty miles in circumference, containing about fifty thousand acres. It has for centuries been the favorite hunting ground of the French monarchs, and is said to be abundantly stocked with game. We could do but little more than admire the strikingly picturesque scenery, in our rambles and drives: but I cannot say we were disturbed by the game, and I hope the game were not disturbed by us. I must add here, by the way, that the New York Central Park is much finer in natural beauty than anything of that character we have yet seen in Europe, and I am almost inclined to assert that these natural advantages have been as skillfully turned to the best account as would have been the case if the work had been in the hands of the most celebrated artists of Europe. So much of the public work in our metropolis is shockingly bungled, and the people's money so shamefully wasted at the same time, that I think the Central Park all the more wonderful, inasmuch as that great work is free from both charges. These remarks are, perhaps, entirely out of place here, but they occurred

to me quite naturally when I was in the Forest of Fontainebleau, and I have as naturally set them down
while writing upon that topic.

Next in order comes a day or two of shopping, but
I know you will not expect any details of what we
did in that way. Yet one little bit of our experience
may furnish a useful hint to future visitors, showing
how necessary it is to be able to judge somewhat of
the actual value of the article sought for. A walking-
stick in one of the fashionable shops attracted my attention, and I enquired the price. "Seventy-five
francs," was the reply. It was so greatly above its
value that I made no offer for it at all. By and bye,
in a shop not quite so elegant, I saw another exactly
like it, evidently from the same manufactory. The
price here was fifty-five francs, but that was still too
high; so I offered forty francs, and, after a good deal
of pathetic talk, which I fortunately did not understand and was therefore entirely unmoved by, the
stick was mine at the price I named. I dare say a
Parisian would have been asked no more than I paid,
and probably would have obtained it for considerably
less. This is only one instance out of many within
my own experience, and much as I hate the practice
of "beating down," I feel bound to recommend a
steady course of it to foreigners in Paris. "English
spoken" is the legend in many of the shop windows,
and "*Prix-fixe*" appears quite as often — the latter
meaning that as the price is fixed to the goods there

is no necessity for asking them at lower figures.
The Guide-Books very highly laud the shops which
adopt this system, and recommend foreigners to deal
where they see "*prix-fixe*" in the windows. This is
a delusion and a snare. It may be true that no out-
rageously exorbitant price is attached to the goods,
but I am certain that many if not all of the dealers
who display that motto expect to take less. Foreigners — Americans especially, and, more especially still,
such of them as cannot speak French — are of course
under great disadvantages in this respect. They enjoy the reputation of having plenty of money and of
not caring much how quickly it is spent. Many are
in the habit of buying things they do not want, because their fancy is taken and the prices look low.
The shop-keepers deal with foreigners upon this pre-
sumption. They show all sorts of articles whether
they are asked for or not, and they have such wheed-
ling ways that it requires some resolution to refuse
to buy. A somewhat ludicrous incident, which was
related to me by an eye-witness, will illustrate the
system of the shop-keepers. A gentleman from Cali-
fornia (I know him very well) went into a fashionable
barber's shop. He could not speak a word of French,
but his signs that he wanted to be shaved and have
his hair trimmed were readily understood. During
the operation the "artist" showed him several handsome brushes, a fine sponge, a variety of different po-
matums and perfumes, a pair of nice razors, and other

toilet articles.   The Californian supposed they simply
wished him to choose what he preferred to be used
upon him.   "How polite these Frenchmen are,"
thought he, and nodded his head, and said " yes,
yes!" to everything, meaning that any of them would
do well enough.   So the barber shaved him with the
new razor, sponged him with the new sponge, oiled
his hair with fresh pomatum and used new combs and
brushes on it, opened several bottles of perfumery
and sprinkled him with them, really doing up the
business, as my friend thought, in a very satisfactory
way.   When he made signs to know what he was to
pay, he was startled with a bill, neatly made out,
amounting to nearly two hundred francs !   The barber had asked him if he would not like to *purchase*
the articles shown, and had understood the Californian to reply in the affirmative, and that he wanted
them tried at once.   The scene which followed may
be easily imagined; it must have been amusing.   An
interpreter had to be procured, and the matter was
finally compromised by the Californian taking such
of the things he had unwittingly bought as were most
damaged in the operation.   But he thinks Paris the
most expensive place to get shaved in that he ever
heard of.

The Père Lachaise is the largest and most celebrated of the cemeteries of Paris.   We spent some hours
in it.   It takes its name from the Jesuit confessor of
Louis XIV., Father Lachaise, who lived in a coun-

try residence on its site. The grounds are about two hundred acres in extent, and though they have been used as a cemetery only about sixty years, the place is now as crowded as any part of old Paris. It is truly "a city of the dead," for it is laid out with paved streets and little sidewalks, very much like the great live city whose dead it shelters. Over the greater portion of the tombs are built little chapels of marble with doors of open iron work or stained glass, and fitted up inside with altar, crucifix and candles, and one or two chairs, according to the size of the chapel. There are, besides, a great many magnificent monuments, but nearly all the graves, except those with only a simple and unpretending head-stone, have the peculiarity I have mentioned. From an eminence at the bank of the cemetery we obtained the finest view of Paris, but in the foreground were the crowded streets of the dead city, suggesting reflections which were, I hope, appropriate to the spot. There are over twenty thousand monuments in the grounds. If I were to undertake to mention the names of eminent personages whose remains repose here, I should have no room left in this letter for anything else. We had only time to visit a few of the most remarkable graves, and I have not room even to speak of all these. The most interesting spot in the place is the tomb of Abélard and Heloïse, which is a Gothic chapel of considerable size, in the style of the thirteenth century, formed out of the ruins of the Abbey of Paraclete, of which Abélard was the founder, and Heloïse the first Abbess. The chapel contains the sarcophagus which was constructed by the order of Abélard, shortly before his death. It represents the ill-fated pair lying side by side. Parisian lovers make it a practice to visit this grave and adorn it with fresh flowers and wreaths; and it was thickly covered with these offerings when we saw it. Nearly all the tombs, indeed, were decorated with flowers and wreaths of yellow immortelles. We walked through the quarter set apart as a burial place for the Jews, and stopped at the tomb of the actress Rachel, which, like so many of the others, was a chapel, though of rather larger size than the average. The walls were entirely covered with names of visitors scratched on the stone, a very unpleasing sight; yet, I dare say, a compliment was intended by every one who took the trouble to make the inscription. I have heard so much of the irreverence of Americans that I expected to see many familiar names, but, I am glad to add, that I discovered none — they were nearly all French. Inside the chapel were many flowers, and the floor was strewed with visiting cards, a fantastic ceremony on the part of visitors which the ghost of the great actress would probably appreciate, but which, to me, had something of mockery in it. There was mockery, too, in the fact that the largest monument in the cemetery, on the highest point of ground, was erected by a wealthy banker to perpetuate his own memory. It is a lofty pyramid, more like a light-house than a monument, and looks down upon the unpretending tombs on which are inscribed the great names of Béranger, Arago, Lafontaine, Molière, Racine, Madame de Genlis, Cherubini, Chopin, Talma, and a host of others famous in literature, the sciences and the arts, whose memory will live long after the massive pile, which is the only record of the wealth and the folly of the mere man of money, has crumbled to dust.

On our way to the cemetery, and on our return, we passed several funeral processions. We stood barehead as the mourners went by, as is the universal custom here. The ceremony never ceases. Eighty interments a day take place in Paris, and more than a third of them are in the Père Lachaise. There are only three cemeteries in the city, and their space would be utterly inadequate to the purpose, if the remains of the poorer classes (two-thirds of the whole number) were not huddled into large pits containing forty or fifty coffins. It costs fifty francs to secure permission to preserve a grave undisturbed for only five years, and five hundred francs for the perpetual right to an extremely limited space, only twenty square feet of ground, hardly sufficient for a single grave. A company has the monopoly of conducting all the funerals, the charges being regulated by official tariff. But enough upon this grave subject.

I wish I could take my readers with me to the great Imperial manufactory of the famous Gobelins Tapes-

try, for I despair of conveying an intelligible idea of
the beauty or of the process of the work. The manufactory is the property of the government, and its
productions are kept for the use of the reigning
monarch, and for presents to foreign courts, princes,
ambassadors and other people of high degree. The
nucleus of the establishment was founded in 1450, by
one Jean Gobelin, who erected a shop for dyeing on
the banks of a little brook, *la Bièvre*, the waters of
which were famous for being peculiarly adapted to
the purpose. His successors combined with the dyeing business the manufacture of tapestry, and in the
course of time their work had attained such high celebrity that Louis XIV. purchased the concern, and
ever since that time it has been operated by the government. Many of the finest productions have been
made during the reign of the present Emperor, and it
is like going into a picture gallery to see the display
of master-pieces. At first sight there is nothing to
distinguish them from the finest oil paintings, except
perhaps a softness and absence of glaze, which are
points certainly in favor of the Gobelins. I will not
undertake to name the remarkable works which are
on exhibition, for I have not been able to find room
for even this much of description when I have spoken
of visits to great picture galleries. There are copies
of celebrated pictures by old masters — copies so fine
as to be worth as much as the originals — but I think
none of the pieces excel in beauty and finish the full-

length portraits of Louis Napoleon and Eugénie, which would deceive certain amateurs of paintings I wot of. The work is done in long galleries, and the men are seen behind the frame on which the warp is stretched from floor to ceiling, selecting the silks and wools from myriads of little bobbins, and comparing them with the subject behind them, which they are copying. The strangest thing about the process to me was that the men do not see the face of the piece whilst they are weaving it. The back of their work is toward them, and the visitors on the outside of the screen see the face of the piece as it progresses. About six square inches is an average day's task, and some idea may be formed from this fact of the great length of time which must be consumed over the largest pieces. The utmost patience and the most practised eye are required. The men must be intelligent and of the superior class — *artists* in fact, though there may be no originality in their works — and I was surprised to learn that their wages ranged as low as two hundred dollars per annum, and never exceeded seven hundred. They look like prisoners whilst at work behind their screens of warp, and it is a mystery to me how men of such skill can be obtained, considering the unpleasantness of the labor and the poverty of its reward.

This is not the place, perhaps, to speak of a picture I saw last week at Versailles, but the thought just here occurs to me to wonder that I did not say some-

thing about it in my last, when speaking of my visit
to the palace at that place, and I must get it off my
mind.   The picture I refer to is the largest I have
ever seen — forty feet in length by sixteen feet in
height.   It is by Horace Vernet, and represents the
capture of the camp of Abdel-Kader by two cavalry
regiments of the French army in 1843.   It is a work
of extraordinary power, and contains numerous portraits.   I have seen a dozen different engravings of
detached groups from this picture.   There is an anecdote current about one of the most effective groups
familiar to most readers, no doubt.   It represents a
most villainous-looking Arab stealing out of one of
the tents and making off with bags of treasure belonging to his master.   The Arab is the living likeness of
the Minister of Finance, M. Fould, and the way he
came to be thus pilloried for all time is related to me
as follows: It appears that he employed Vernet to
paint his portrait, but tried to make the great painter
abate something on his price when it was done, on
the ground that the likeness was not correct.   The
master refused to take less than the sum he originally
named, and M. Fould spoke of rejecting the work.
"Very well," said Vernet, "it is not your picture
now, but mine; and as you say it is not like you I
will exhibit it."   And exhibit it he did, having transferred the features to the figure of the thieving Arab
in the great picture he was then at work upon.   The
likeness which M. Fould demurred at is recognized

by every one who looks at the picture and is familiar
with the original, and those who are not are pretty
sure, like myself, to be told the story. There was an
eccentricity about the painter's method of revenge
which savored of madness, as it seems to me — but
the madness which is akin to genius, I suppose.

I am drawing near to the end of the space to which
I limit each letter, and there are many things I expected to describe to you yet unmentioned. But you
have got used by this time to my habit of running a
variety of matters into a small space at the end, and
will not therefore be surprised to find this letter
wound up in a somewhat similarly abrupt fashion.
Learn, then, briefly, that we found time the past
week to visit the Jardin d'acclimatation, in the Bois
de Boulogne, where experiments are being made, and
successfully too, to acclimatize foreign plants, animals,
and birds in great variety. There is a great aqua-
rium, also, with ten glass reservoirs filled with sea
water and four with fresh, all constantly renewed by
means of pumps, and containing a most interesting
collection of beautiful fishes and queer fishes, all apparently enjoying life as well as though in their
native homes. The grounds of the garden are tastefully laid out, and there are cages and inclosures
for the four-footed inmates as little like prisons as
possible. I will not pretend to tell the number of
different birds and animals, and foreign plants, flowers
and shrubs that are here exhibited in all their na-

tive health and vigor; but I know it appeared to me a very wonderful thing to see representatives of the vegetable and animal life of every clime grouped in this comparatively small space; and when I learned in addition, that the various seeds, eggs, and young animals could be purchased at moderate prices at the " bureau," I could not help thinking how well they do these things in France.

The Jardin des Plantes also merited a much longer visit than we could devote to it, for it contains apparently almost every object connected with the natural sciences which the student could wish for.   From its name we might infer that it is specially devoted to botany, but the horticultural department, though very extensive, is not more important than the zoological museum and garden, the cabinet of comparative anatomy, or the geological department, which are connected with it.   Lectures by fifteen different Professors, men of the highest celebrity, are given in an amphitheatre capable of holding twelve hundred persons, and the public have gratuitous admission to them.

I do not like to quit Paris without saying something about the Great Palace which is now being erected for the Universal Exposition of 1867. We drove around the outside of the building, and I think it must have been a journey of at least two miles, perhaps much more. The plan is beautifully simple, yet I have not space to describe it. How it is to be finished by the time stated is more than I can conceive, but the Emperor has said it shall be done, so I suppose it will. Nothing is impossible in Paris — say Parisians — and if the plan which I have seen of the buildings and grounds is carried out by next April, I shall believe the boast.

It seems to me that I have written a good deal about Paris, considering that I have been here only two weeks — at least I have taken up considerable space about it; but when I reflect upon how much I have seen of which I have not spoken at all I am quite dissatisfied with my work. If I do write you any more about Paris, however, it must be in a future letter, for it is near midnight now, and we start at six o'clock to-morrow morning for London.

IX.

HORRORS OF CROSSING THE CHANNEL. — VAIN CONFIDENCE
AND WHAT CAME OF IT. — SUFFERINGS FROM SEA-SICK-
NESS. — THE ROUTE FROM PARIS TO DIEPPE, THENCE TO
NEWHAVEN. — ENGLAND AT LAST. — RURAL SCENERY OF
ENGLAND COMPARED WITH THAT OF THE CONTINENT. —
LONDON. — A WEEK OF SIGHT-SEEING, INCLUDING VISITS
TO PARKS, PICTURE GALLERIES, THE CRYSTAL PALACE,
THEATRES, THE TOWER, ETC.

LONDON, August 14th, 1866.

It sometimes happens that a man begins to crow
like chanticleer before the victory is won, and the
present writer lately was very unpleasantly reminded
that to do this is to do a very foolish thing.   Thus it
was: You remember, I dare say, that in my first letter I mentioned with something of exultation the fact
that though I was touched I was not conquered by
sea-sickness on my voyage out. I don't think I said
a great deal about it to you, but I must now admit
that I have lately bragged not a little over my escape
when I have been speaking on the subject to friends
who inquired about my experience in crossing the

Atlantic. I have claimed to be a good sailor, for whom sea-sickness had no terrors; and when I was warned that crossing the Channel was a trip which was dreaded by the most seasoned travelers, I made light of it, affirming that it could not bring an " old salt " like myself to grief. It was in this confident frame of mind that I embarked at Dieppe for New-haven, the day after I finished my last letter, just a week ago. The weather was disagreeable, and some-thing of a sea was on, according to the sailors, but nothing unusual or alarming. I noticed that nearly all the passengers found places to lie down in the lit-tle saloons almost before the boat had left the wharf, only a few over-confident ones, like myself, being de-termined to weather it out on deck. In less than a quarter of an hour, however, I found the weather too much for me, and went below. Trouble had already begun, and I had hardly done the little it was possi-ble to do for those who needed my services before I found it expedient to lie down myself. I noticed that at every man's head a large white bowl was standing, but yet I was rather indignant when the steward's boy placed one in front of me. "I shall not need it," said I. " *Won't* you, sir? " responded the boy, with an incredulous emphasis on the first word, darting off, as he spoke, with a fresh bowl to an unfortunate gentleman who had been in very evident distress from the first moment of the voyage, and just then, after terrible groaning and retching, with a single

7

violent gush, filled his first basin. The boy had very
little peace after that until the voyage was ended. I
watched him as he ran about, changing basins in response to the agonized calls of "steward! steward!"
and, I grieve to add, the boy watched me as well.
His post was at the cabin door, and what time he got
to stand there he employed in looking at me, eager, I
could see, to serve me with a fresh basin. The study
of my face in the hope to discover symptoms of coming woe, appeared to have a peculiar fascination for
him, for I never looked up but I caught his malignant
eye upon me.

Soon I began to feel a dreadful commotion within
me, and I know my face became of a deathly greenish-
white hue, for I saw a half-satisfied but yet expectant
smile steal over that fiendish boy's countenance. This
put me upon my mettle, and I determined to disappoint him or perish in the attempt. With a mighty
effort I kept down the rising storm in the interior,
and fought off the green sea-monster during five
or six long hours; but the agony I endured must forever remain untold from sheer inability to adequately
describe the sensations of smothered sea-sickness. I
freely admit that I should have felt better had I suc-
cumbed to the storm, but my pride was aroused, and
I would not — in short, throw up — whilst that evil-
eyed boy was watching me. Three or four times I
attempted to rise and make my way upon deck, but I
could not stand the motion, and had to plump down

very quickly every time I tried it. At length we
were within an hour of reaching our haven, and I began to feel confident of victory. Thought I would
make a sure thing of it, by trying the remedy I boast-
ed of so much in my first letter, and therefore sipped
down a tumbler of champagne which I had not felt
equal to until then. Some one looked out of a window and said we were nearly at the dock. I jumped
up to look after my companions and baggage, and —
(fancy my feelings when I was so nearly triumphant!) — fell back again so deathly and so suddenly
sick that I had barely time to grasp the obnoxious
bowl which had stood before me so long. "Have a
fresh basin, sir?" said that horrible boy, who was at
my head in a moment. "*Knew* you'd want one, sir,"
he added with quiet malignity. I was too sick to reply, and could not even look one of my looks at him.
But I did want to break his head for him, the young
villain.

It was only a single spurt though, after all — nothing but the champagne — and in a few moments I felt
so nice and quiet within that my resentment all van-
ished, and I heaped a shilling's worth of coals of fire
upon the poor boy's head, much to his surprise, as I
thankfully passed out of the cabin on my way to the
shore.

I know right well that I ought not to have commenced this letter with a recital of my unpleasant experiences in crossing the Channel, if I would continue

to pursue the plan I have followed in my previous letters — I mean that of narrating the incidents of travel
in regular order as they occurred, — but I was so impressed with the fear that I was enjoying an unde-
served reputation as "a good sailor" with such of
my readers as do not quite forget what I scribble
about — and another fear that I might possibly have
been instrumental in inducing other voyagers to place
an undue reliance upon the virtues of champagne as a
remedy against sea-sickness — that I thought it best
to lose no time in correcting these false impressions.
But I will now go back to Paris (without crossing
that dreadful Channel again, though, I thank heaven!)
and bring you who kindly accompany me from thence
to London by "the pleasantest summer route" according to Guide-Books and advertisements.

The quotation in the last sentence — with the fact
that it is, at the same time, certainly much cheaper
than by the way of Calais and Dover — will explain
why I took the route from Paris to London via
Dieppe and Newhaven. I can cheerfully endorse all
that is claimed for the land part of the journey, and I
cannot aver that there is not just as much sea-sickness
to be endured in the shorter passage over the Channel from Calais to Dover as in the longer one that we
traveled. In pleasant weather the latter is said to be
a much smoother way than the former, and I think
that much very likely is true; but pleasant weather is
the exception, rough weather the rule, in the Channel,

and the sea passage is four or five hours longer from
Dieppe to Newhaven than from Calais to Dover
(though there is generally only about two hours' difference in favor of the latter route, taking the entire
journey between Paris and London) — therefore, after what I have said of the horrors of this "middle
passage," I think it will be readily inferred that it
must be a very fine day indeed that would tempt me
to choose the longer sea route again, though it is so
much the cheapest. Admitting that one will as surely
be sick, and as severely sick, the other way, there is
only one-third of the time to be sick in; and I know
that when the two-thirds of our sea journey was still
to be endured we would gladly have paid twice the
money we saved if we could have saved that distance.
You must not fancy, either, that this writer was the
sickest man on board. Far from it. He was well, at
peace, contented, happy — nay, jolly even — compared with some of his fellow wretches. Everybody was
sick — some so desperately sick that it seemed they
would wrench themselves to pieces. — — But here I
am, back again upon this dreadful topic, sea-sickness!
I am sure I don't know why I harp upon it so. It is
certainly anything but a pleasant subject. I will
leave it now, for good.

On our way from Paris to Dieppe we passed through
Rouen, an old, important and very interesting town,
at which I would advise travelers to stop at least a
day. It has now over one hundred thousand inhabi-

tants, was the ancient capital of Normandy, and has more and richer specimens of mediæval architecture than any other city in France. Its Cathedral is a grand Gothic edifice, one of the finest on the continent, and has many interesting relics. One of its chapels contains the tomb of Rollo, the first Duke of Normandy, who died in 927; in another there is an old mutilated figure of Richard the Lion-heart, of England, who died in 1199. This figure was discovered in 1838, and the heart of the great Crusader was found at the same time, and is now preserved in the Museum, which contains many other curious relics, old documents, etc., one of the latter bearing the sign-manuel (a cross) of William the Conqueror, who died in this town. Beautiful as is the Cathedral, Rouen can boast a still finer Gothic Church, the Abbey of St. Ouen, which was founded in 1318, added to at different periods, and has only recently been entirely completed; but the original plan having been closely followed, there is a rare harmony of design throughout the entire edifice. It surpasses the Cathedral in extent and chasteness of style, and the people of Rouen claim that it is one of the few perfect Gothic structures in the world. Tradition asserts that the architect of this noble church, Alexander Berneval, killed his apprentice in a fit of jealousy, because his execution of the rose window of the north transept gave proof of a skill that surpassed the master's. It was in this town that Joan of Arc was burned at the stake,

in 1431. The spot on which she suffered is now occupied by a fountain.

The route from Paris to Dieppe affords much beautiful scenery. It winds along the valley of the Seine,
which is crossed more than a score of times in the
journey. There are many old towns on the line, at
every one of which incidents of historical interest
have occurred. If the traveler can afford time to
make many stops, he may visit the town of Poissy,
where Saint Louis was born; Mantes, where William
the Conqueror fell from his horse and received the injury of which he died; the Tower of Vernon, where
Philip Augustus of France found refuge when conquered by Richard Cœur de Lion; the ruins of the
Castle of Gaillard, near Les Andelys, where Margaret
of Burgundy was strangled by order of her husband,
Louis X.; and many other points of interest may be
found by the persevering and leisurely traveler.

Dieppe, where we took the steamer for Newhaven,
is quite a fashionable watering-place. The Emperor
pays frequent visits to it, and it is the annual resort
of many English and French families, who come to
enjoy the splendid sea-bathing which the place affords.
In front of the bathing establishment there are about
two hundred little tents, from which the bathers de-
scend into the water, presenting a very novel and animated scene when the weather is fine and the season
is at the height. One of the greatest curiosities of
Dieppe is a great oyster park, where the bivalves,

first brought from the inexhaustible beds near Cherbourg, are dieted in a way which is said to materially improve their flavor. The markets of Paris are principally supplied from this source.

But I must quit these details and hasten over to England, where, an inward monitor reminds me, I ought to have taken you long ago. Having already told something about the six hours' passage across the Channel, and having promised to say no more about sea-sickness, it is but a jump and there we are, on the grand old Island, where everything looks so beautifully green, so comfortable and homelike, that I feel almost inclined to throw myself upon the broad bosom of the dear old Mother-land, and kiss her still fair fresh face! How pleasant it sounds to me, too, the good old English tongue, after these months of wrestling with foreign lingoes! And I am strongly inclined to shake hands with the honest porter, who is the first man to speak to me in England.

There is little or no trouble with the customs officers on arriving in England. So few articles are liable to duty that the examination of baggage has become almost a mere form. Tobacco is subject to a high impost, and travelers are generally asked if they have any of that obnoxious weed about their persons or luggage. Not a fourth of my bags or boxes were even looked into, though I unlocked them all quite readily. The best way is to open everything to inspection cheerfully, and then you will get along nicely, as the officers are not apt to put themselves to unnecessary trouble in pulling your things about merely for the sake of annoying you. Of course they are at liberty to take everything out of your trunks, if they choose; but I have always found that civility begets civility, and if you are disposed to make things pleasant yourself you will find few public officials who are not ready to second your efforts. I go into this subject at the greater length, because I know from my own experience that a good deal of unfounded dread of trouble with the customs inspectors exists among travelers. I only hope I shall have as little trouble in that direction with our own authorities, on my return, as I have found in Europe.

The first thing which strikes an American who has been traveling on the Continent before reaching England, is the totally different and far more beautiful aspect of the rural scenery in the latter country. This is not due so much to a higher state of cultivation of the soil, perhaps, as to the different method of dividing the fields. On the Continent hedges and fences are unknown. The land is cut up into little narrow patches and planted with different productions, quite close to each other, without even a trench to divide them. In many places there is no protection from the public highways, the land being cultivated up to the edge of the road. This gives the face of the country a curious appearance. It looks, when seen from a distance, as though the land was covered

7*

with a huge striped carpet.   In England the fields are
separated by thick, flowery hedges.   Handsome trees,
sometimes alone, sometimes in little clumps, are left
standing to make the scene more picturesque.   In the
corners of many fields are little ponds of water.   Long,
narrow, crooked lanes, in which the hedges nearly
meet overhead, lead to the broader highroads.   The
whole country, indeed, often looks as though it were
laid out by a skillful landscape gardener.   There is no
question that the Continental system of farming has a
great advantage over that which prevails in England,
in a utilitarian point of view.   Not an inch of space is
left uncultivated with the former, whilst with the latter the trees, hedges, ditches and lanes, must take
out a large slice of the productive capacity of the soil.
But there is also no question about which system pre-
serves the face of Nature in the fairest aspect.   In
England the denizen of a man-made town realizes at
once that God made the country; on the Continent
the hand of man is almost as visible in the country as
in the city, so mathematically are the lines of the
fields laid down.   The title to the land in England is
seldom vested in the farmers.   Great proprietors, the
hereditary aristocracy, are the owners of the soil, and
farms are leased upon stringent conditions as to preserving the timber and cultivating the hedges; otherwise it is hardly possible but that beauty would be
sacrificed to utility, and the Continental agricultural
system come into vogue in England where land is so
valuable.

You may be sure, however, that we did not bother our heads with speculations of this nature upon our journey from Newhaven to London. We were too thankful that we were upon the solid earth again, and too much occupied in admiring the beautiful country to care for the whys and wherefores of the question. A civil "guard" (whose civility was not inadequately rewarded, I hope,) gave us a coach to ourselves on the railway, procured us a cab and attended to the loading of our baggage when we arrived at the station; and we found ourselves pleasantly located in a comfortable hotel, in the West End of London, without the least trouble, and not so late in the evening but that a good supper of the best mutton-chops we ever tasted was as wholesome as it was welcome.

Here we are then, in London at last, and here we have been about a week. The time has not been idled away, I can assure you; indeed I have been so constantly occupied one way and another that I have had no leisure for writing, and begrudge the time which must be given to this letter. I am glad to think that you will not expect particular details of what we see in London, knowing as much already about most of the sights as I could write you were time and space less limited than they are. I shall only trouble you, therefore, with the briefest mention of what we have "done" thus far.

The first day was nearly all needed for rest, but we managed to find energy enough in the latter part of

it for three or four hours' drive about the streets and
in the Parks.   It is not "the season" now in London,
as I need not tell you, and there is not much of the
fashionable world to be seen in Regent and Oxford
streets, or in the Parks.   So we are told, and yet we
thought the scene a very gay one.   We drove about
Hyde Park where the late riots occurred, and saw
more than a mile of high board fence which had been
erected in place of the strong iron paling that was
forced down by the crowd.   It is hard to say whether
the authorities were not more to blame than the riot-
ers, so different are the views of the newspapers.
They are accused of showing too much leniency by
one class, and of trampling on the rights of the people
by another.   One thing is very certain: a crowd of
London "roughs" is the most brutal crowd that
can be brought together in any place in the world,
and I find many sensible people here who believe that
military force will have to be more frequently resorted
to than formerly to keep down the disorderly classes
of the great city.   There is everywhere in England
such a jealous regard for the rights of the people that
the idea is not a popular one, but it seems to me in-
evitable that the Government must strengthen itself
in some way, or else fall at no very distant day before
the power of King Mob.

We thought the pictures of the Foreign School in
the National Gallery rather a meagre display, and the
building a contracted, shabby affair, after seeing the

immense collections and the magnificent palaces in which they are housed, on the Continent. There are some priceless gems of the old masters in the Gallery, but not many, comparatively. One entire room is devoted to the pictures of the eccentric J. M. W. Turner, and it seemed to me that the pictures were more eccentric than the painter. His style resembles no other artist's, living or dead. A "Turner" will be recognized as far as it can be seen, but I must confess that I cannot rank myself among the admirers of this master. I gave the paintings a somewhat attentive examination, and tried hard to come to a different conclusion, for I had so greatly admired engravings which I had seen of his works that I expected to be delighted with the originals; but it was of no use — I could not help thinking that a majority of the paintings looked like the works of a madman. Of course there must be great merit in them, or they would not be so highly valued; only my taste is not educated up to the capacity for appreciation. Upon this point I freely write myself down an ass.

Very different was the feeling with which I viewed other great works of the British School now temporarily exhibited at the Kensington Museum. There are the splendid pictures of Sir Edwin Landseer, with which the whole world is familiar through engravings. But no engraving can convey an idea of the exquisite finish and yet wonderful strength of the originals. You would like to spend a day with " Alexander and

Diogenes," a group of eight dogs — surly old Diogenes in his kennel looking at magnificent Alexander
and his obsequious train of curs and courtiers of every
degree, as much as to say "stand out of the sunshine,
if you would do me a favor;" — with the "Maid and
the Magpie" — with "Low Life and High Life" —
"Dignity and Impudence" — "Peace" and "War"
— "The Hunted Stag" — "Highland Music" — "A
dialogue at Waterloo," the latter a great picture representing the old Iron Duke and the present Duchess
of Wellington on horseback at the field of Waterloo,
where the hero has been fighting the battle over
again, ending by saying to his companion "but 'twas
a famous victory;" — these and a score others of
Landseer's famous pictures, familiar as household
words, are in the Gallery at Kensington. There too
are the great originals of Hogarth's dramatic pictures,
masterpieces by Wilkie, Gainsborough, Reynolds,
West, Lawrence, Jackson, Maclise, Leslie, Stanfield,
Herring, Frith, Rosa Bonheur, and a host of others,
to admire which one does not have to put on a wise
air and pretend to discover points of excellence he
knows nothing about, as he does when looking at too
many of the works of the old masters. The merits
of these pictures speak to you at once in tones you
are familiar with.   .

We have spent a day at the Crystal Palace of Sydenham, but there was so much to see, such a crowd
of people, such beautiful grounds and walks and foun-

tains, such a wonderful collection of works of art, so many different courts, models of antique rooms, and specimens of gigantic tropical plants and trees all growing in their native vigor in the wonderful Glass Palace — more astonishing than anything dreamed of in the "Arabian Nights" — that the impression left on my mind is all confused, and I can give no description of the place whatever. In the evening there was a display of such gorgeous fireworks as I never saw before, or any approach to them indeed, and we returned at night fairly exhausted with admiration. If I can give another day to the Palace I will try and keep cool and collected enough to be able to tell you something about it. And yet you know I am not given to an over-indulgence in enthusiasm.

We have visited two of the most celebrated theatres, the "Haymarket" and the "Adelphi." Here there was disappointment. The first is a dingy little place, hardly as large as our "Metropolitan," and not half as pretty. The Adelphi is somewhat larger than the Haymarket, but still is not equal to any of the first-class theatres of our metropolis, either in size or elegance. "The Fast Family," a rather exciting but very improbable play, adapted from the French, is having a long run here. The famous comedians, Paul Bedford and J. L. Toole, were in the piece, but I confess that I should not have known they were great actors had I not seen their names in the bill. This, however, is very likely due to the fact that I did not

see them in any of their favorite parts. Bedford is a
very portly old man, with a splendid voice, and reminds one strongly of John Gilbert, of Wallack's, but
I think the latter much the better actor. Don't think,
however, that I mean to be critical, for that would be
absurd under the circumstances. Mrs. Alfred Mellon
had the best part in the piece, and she certainly did
ample justice to it. The afterpiece was an extrava-
ganza and spectacle-operatic affair, called "Helen, or
taken from the Greeks," but I could not sit it out.
Such dreary puns, and such stupid nonsense, I could
not endure. About a week before I had seen "Cin-
derella" at the Grand Chatelet Theatre in Paris.
It was a ballet, an opera, a comedy and a magnificent spectacle combined in one. Perhaps this gorgeous entertainment had spoiled me for any other
production of that kind. It was truly wonderful.
Put together all that I had ever seen before in that
line, and the sum would not make up the half of what
was shown me in this one piece. The "Chatelet" is
an immense theatre, and seats nearly four thousand
people. It has seven tiers of boxes, so you may imagine what a height they have for effects on the stage.
But I forget, I am not writing about Paris now.

And yet one who comes from Paris to London can
hardly avoid drawing a comparison between the two
cities, and not often, I must confess, so far as appearances go, in favor of the latter. The streets and
buildings of the new Paris are so much more elegant

than anything in London that the latter is quite an old-fashioned dingy city in comparison. The buildings of London, even on the finest streets, are so low that they make a poor show, and this is the case with structures of quite modern date. Few are over three or four stories high, and the ground-floors are seldom more than ten or twelve feet between joists. The finest buildings of Regent and Oxford streets are of this character, the fashion being attributed to George the Fourth, in whose reign many of them were erected. The "first gentleman in Europe" would not hear of more than three stories to any building with which he had to do. Perhaps "your fat friend" had constitutional objections to stairs. Well, there is something in that, too. Alas, that candor compels me to admit it!

We went to Her Majesty's Theatre one evening, a really magnificent place, and spacious as well. The orchestra was grand, but there were few of the vocal performers whom I had not heard excelled in the Academy at New York. I except Mad'lle Titiens, who is a prima donna charming in every way. Mr. Tom Hohler was the tenor. He is a nice-looking chap, as our musical critic would say, but not much of a singer.

By far the most interesting place we have yet visited is the Tower of London, where we spent two or three hours under the guidance of a very entertaining but pragmatical old "beef-eater," who had

"sarved George the Third when a' was a lad," as he
informed us every five minutes. We were shown the
block upon which three Queens — Anne Boleyn,
Catharine Howard and Lady Jane Grey — were beheaded, and held the fatal axe in our hands. There
was one dent in the block deeper than the rest, and
we fancied it was made when the head of that poor
lady who had such "a little neck" was taken off. I
shall not enumerate what we saw — everybody knows
what is to be seen in the Tower. The old "beef-
eater," however, did not assume that we knew anything about anything. "Look here, young ladies and
gentlemen," he would say, "did iver ye read about
Sir Walter Raleigh? Well, this is the room where
he was confined for siven years. There, now, what
do you say to that?" And then he would march on
to some other object and demand again "did iver ye
read," or "did iver ye hear tell," before he told us
what it was. He was a nice old fellow though, and
did his very best, and I hope he did not repent it
when we went away. We were most interested in
the room called the Beauchamp Tower, where the
State prisoners were formerly confined. The walls
are covered with inscriptions, many of them of great
interest. There is one over the fire-place, peculiarly
affecting. It runs thus: "*The more suffering for
Christ in this world — the more glory with Christ in
the next. Thou has crowned him with honour and
glory, O Lord! In memory everlasting He will be*

just. ARUNDELL, *June 22nd*, 1587." This inscription
was made by the unfortunate Philip Howard, son of
that Duke of Norfolk who was beheaded by Elizabeth
for aspiring to marry Mary Queen of Scots. Philip's
offence was his religion, he being a devoted Romanist.
He was imprisoned in this room many years, and was
only released a short time before his death. But the
most interesting inscription we found was the word
" IANE," said to be the work of Lord Guilford Dud-
ley, the husband of the unhappy Lady Jane Grey. A
description of these inscriptions would more than fill
one of my letters, so I may as well stop here, especially as my allotted space is nearly filled up already.

I had intended to say something about the " Street
Cries " of London, but I have not the room now. Besides, I don't understand any of them as yet. There
is one old fellow who passes my window as regularly
as the clock, but what he has to sell I cannot guess.
His cry has three notes, like the croak of a raven,
and I am very curious to know what it means. If I
can get up early enough some morning to waylay
him, I will find it out and write you about it.

More home friends. Mr. and Mrs. J. S. have been
with us the last three or four days. They were in
Scotland when they heard of our arrival here, and ran
down to visit us. They left for Paris this evening,
expecting to see the Emperor's great *fête* to-morrow.
With this local item, for which I expect your thanks,
I bid you good-bye for the present.

X.

LONDON. — DIFFICULTIES IN THE WRITER'S WAY. — A VISIT
TO ST. PAUL'S AND SOME REFLECTIONS UPON THE MONEY-
CHANGERS IN THAT TEMPLE. — A GOSSIP WITH THE OLD
LADY OF THREADNEEDLE STREET. — MADAME TUSSAUD'S
WAX-WORK SHOW. — THE ZOOLOGICAL GARDENS. — STREET
SIGHTS. — A DIGRESSION.

LONDON, August 24th, 1866.

London is "too many" for your correspondent.
He neither knows where to begin when he wants to
tell your readers of its sights and wonders, nor where
to stop when he does make a beginning. The consequence is that he feels no confidence of being able to
do anything, except the thing of all others he least
desires to do, namely, tire the patience of the indul-
gent friends who read his letters at the same time
that he is exhausting his own. Reflecting upon this
almost certain contingency leads him to meditate put-
ting an abrupt end to these "Notes of European
Travel," as you have so kindly christened his rambling letters; or rather, to put no end to them at all

and let them stop with the last, so that you would be as much surprised at the conclusion as you were at the beginning; which would be consistent, to say the least.

Seriously, the trouble which afflicts me (I must speak in the first person on so purely personal a matter) when I sit down to write to you, is that I have too much to say and too little time to say it in. I have complained of this in some of my former letters and I dare say enough has been said on that point; but here, in this vast metropolis, the difficulty is so much more intense than ever before that I must speak of it again, or burst. Of course it is not entirely without motive that I am so earnest. If I can succeed in stamping upon the minds of my readers a fair impression of the disadvantages under which I write, they will the more leniently judge my work; and I am very sure the widest cloak of charity will be required to cover the multitude of sins which might be discovered in my letters by the mildest of critics. One feels very little like writing, I assure you, in the evening after a day's sight-seeing; and less still like taking a whole day to it when there is so much yet to be "done," and time is so limited and so very costly. It has required all the perseverance for which I so frequently claim credit to bring me to the point of writing lately, as you may have discovered, perhaps, when a rather longer interval than usual has passed between my letters. But this present is begun with greater reluctance than any of its predecessors. I only hope the hard writing will not prove equally hard reading.

Well (to make a beginning), I must say something about our visit to St. Paul's Cathedral. Several days have passed since that event, but they have not been sufficient to efface the feeling of disappointment with which I emerged from that immense edifice. I could hardly realize that I had been inside a church, so little was there to inspire that feeling of religious awe which is proper to the place. No doubt this feeling arose from the fact that I had become disgusted with the mercenary spirit which appears to preside over the place. There is free admission to the body of the Cathedral, around which, in niches and on the walls, are erected beautiful monuments to the memory of many of England's departed worthies. There are no seats in this part of the great temple, and it more resembles, both from the immensity of the space and the character of the architecture, a public hall or exchange than a House of God. If one had not received this impression at the first entrance he would soon be helped to it — "by order of the Dean and Chapter," I presume — if his experience was like mine. We were in front of one of the finest memorials when an official approached and asked if we did not wish to buy tickets of admission to the other parts of the church. "By and by," I replied, "after we have seen this part." We passed along to another monument, that of gruff old Sam. Johnson, I think;—and very queer he looked, with nothing on him but a robe arranged after the classic Greek fashion—I could not help fancying how tremendously he would have stormed if any one had proposed such a dress for him when he was in the flesh! Whilst we were standing there, recalling familiar incidents in the life of the stout old Doctor, another fellow came and solicited us to buy some tickets. Him we paid no attention to. A vision of the burly lexicographer was before me at the moment, knocking down the bookseller with a copy of his big dictionary, and I could not help wishing that his ghost would dispose of the intrusive touter in a similar summary way. But we kept on, quietly and leisurely examined all the monuments that were accessible to us, not without noticing, also, the placards which were frequently and conspicuously posted, giving a tariff of the charges for admission to the different parts of the Cathedral. At length we bought tickets to the vaults, another active drummer having persuaded us (now that we were ready) that it was worth our while. We stumbled down a dark pair of stairs, and were soon groping our way about the vaults, which are only lighted here and there by grated windows. We found the tomb of Sir Christopher Wren, the architect of St. Paul's, and the tombs of many other eminent men, without assistance; but were beginning to think we should have to give up the search for those of Nelson and Wellington, which are the main attraction, when a dapper little fellow came out with a party of visitors from one of the aisles into which we had tried in vain to enter, the door being fastened. As we had been stumbling we were still grumbling, whereupon he promptly informed us that it was the custom for people to wait at the foot of the dark stairs, until "a husher" could attend to them. We submitted to the rebuke in silence, and then the "husher" took our tickets and conducted us into a vault where the ashes of England's two greatest heroes repose. In a horrid cockney dialect he gave us the particulars of the tombs. There is nothing remarkable about Nelson's tomb. Wellington's is a splendid sarcophagus of brown stone, of immense size and weight. It is surrounded by captured battle-flags, regalia, and the funereal trappings which were used when the great captain was buried. The funeral car, which was cast from cannon taken by the Duke in some of his battles, is here preserved, and harnessed to it are models of the black horses which drew it in the procession, "hexackly like the horiginals," as our guide informed us. I should perhaps have thought it a splendid resting place for the departed hero, if I had not so recently visited the tomb of his mighty opponent at the Invalides, in Paris. France has placed the ashes of Napoleon in so grand a temple that the tomb to which England has consigned all that was mortal of Wellington looks a poor affair by comparison. Napoleon's tomb is lighted from the great dome of the Invalides, and France invites all the world freely to visit the shrine. Wellington's tomb is in a dark cellar, and England charges all the world "sixpence a head" for a sight of it. All the world thinks England might forego the sixpence without loss of honor, though it might involve a slight sacrifice of profit.

Ascending again, we paid some more sixpences for tickets to the Whispering Gallery round the base of the great dome. Two hundred and eighty steps took us up, where an old female in a greasy black dress, and bonnet to match, took our tickets and directed us to take seats about half way round the Gallery where some other visitors were sitting. By-and-bye, when a few more had come up so as to make it worth her while, she told us to hold our heads close to the wall, and then she whispered some particulars about the Cathedral which we heard very distinctly though we were nearly two hundred feet distant from her. The effect was very curious, the sound being as if the words were spoken in our ears, and in a much louder tone than the speaker used. The old woman was so very curt and disagreeable that I believe no one solicited her to break the rule which was printed on the tickets, forbidding her to accept any gratuity; but she looked as though she thought us "a shabby lot" for omitting to do so.

We might have gone higher and seen more, by buy-

8

ing some more tickets, but the stairs were too many, and we didn't want to spend the time—or the money. In truth, I was completely disgusted at the business-like air and grasping, avaricious spirit which were manifested on all sides. We hurried down stairs, found the touters still busy soliciting visitors to procure tickets for the paying parts of the show, and went out of St. Paul's without the slightest impression, as I said before, that we had been in a Christian church, but heartily praying that the day might soon come when the Money-changers should be driven out of that Temple. I give no details about the noble structure, knowing that its general features and history are familiar to all readers. I prefer in this case, as I have frequently done in others, to give the experience and impressions of a sight-seer, rather than particulars which may be obtained in any Hand-Book. But I must not forget to note that one is almost sure to be disappointed at the first near view of this magnificent Cathedral, for it is so crowded on all sides with buildings that it is impossible to realize a correct idea of its vastness and beautiful proportions. Yet if the stranger sees it many times, as I have done, and tries to look at it from all points, he will admit that Londoners may well be proud of their Cathedral; and that its builder deserves that it should be called his monument. Do you remember the inscription which is cut on the plain marble slab erected to his memory over the entrance to the Choir? It is in

Latin, of which the following is a translation : " Be-
"neath lies Sir Christopher Wren, the builder
"of this Church and City, who lived upwards of
"ninety years, not for himself, but for the public
"good. Reader, seekest thou his monument ? Look
"around ! "

When I tell you that we have paid a visit to the
"Old Lady of Threadneedle Street," you will understand that I was favored with a Visitor's Card to the
Bank of England. No one but the Governor, or his
Deputy, I was informed, could grant this favor, and
it is not so easy as formerly to obtain the desired permission. A banking gentleman, with whom I had
business, and who is also a Director in the Bank of
England, was kind enough to procure me the card,
which admitted five persons; but I know he had to
send several times before he could get it, and I was
beginning to feel very sorry I had put him to the
trouble. He said that visits caused such an interrup-
tion of business that the Governor was obliged to
be more chary of his permits. There are only three
days in the week when an inspection of the institution
is allowed. Of course this difficulty gave additional
value to the privilege when it was obtained, and we
were quite prepared to be awe-struck as we entered
the building. A big porter, attired in gorgeous scar-
let livery embroidered with gold lace, ushered us into
the Bank, and another conducted us to a little private
waiting room, where the sole ornament was an en-

graved likeness of the Bank's first governor. Here
we were requested to be seated, while the porter took
our card to an inner sanctuary. Very soon a little
lame old chap in buff livery came to us. He looked
as though he might have been in the Old Lady's service ever since his childhood, and undoubtedly was
put upon this sort of light work because of his in-
firmity. He requested me to inscribe my name and
residence, and the name of the person by whom I had
been introduced, in the visitors' book, and, this done,
conducted us through the most interesting rooms of
the vast establishment. It took nearly two hours to
give a hurried glance at what he had to show, and I
regret that space is not accorded me for a full description of the wonders which were unfolded to us.

In the first room to which we were conducted we
saw self-acting machines at work weighing endless
piles of sovereigns, passing those of full weight into
one receptacle, and kicking the light ones into another. At certain intervals the attendants pour out
the correct coins into measures, and the defective ones
are taken to a machine which defaces them at the rate
of two hundred a minute, so that they cannot be used
again. All the sovereigns which are paid into the
Bank in large quantities pass through this ordeal, and
the light ones are returned to the depositor or taken
at their value as old gold. I think there were at least
a dozen of these weighing machines at work, and
when I tell you that nearly fifty a minute are passed

through each, a very little mental arithmetic will give you an idea of the enormous amount of money which is sometimes tested in this room in a single day.

In another room we saw a bigger pile of Mexican silver dollars than you could dream of. A score of clerks were busy counting them, and the chief man told us that three millions of these nice solid-looking coins had been received from Mexico within a week. I presume they were to pay the interest on some Mexican bonds. I would have liked a few bushels of them, and could hardly believe that so small a quantity would be missed. We were allowed to handle some bricks of pure gold, weighing about fourteen pounds each, and it occurred to me that one might be excused for wishing to have "a brick in his hat" of that sort.

We went into another and larger room, crowded with desks, where about fifty clerks were hard at work examining and defacing bank notes. You know, I presume, that the Bank of England never re-issues one of its notes. When they are first sent out upon their travels a record of each individual note is made, and by a process of consecutive numbering no two notes are exactly alike. As soon as they return home they are compared with the record, scrutinized to detect forgeries, mutilated, and then put away where they can be found at any moment for ten years to come. Not one of them is permitted to try a second course of adventures. Many, of course, come back

the same day, just as clean and fresh and crisp as
when they went out in the morning; but they are
treated quite as harshly as those which are brought
back in a ragged, dirty, disreputable-looking condition, after traveling all over the world and partici-
pating in the dissipations of all countries. Notes to
the amount of more than a million pounds sterling
were cancelled on the day we visited the Bank. It
seemed a pity to see so much nice-looking money —
good for its face anywhere — so ruthlessly destroyed;
but such is the system of the Old Lady of Threadneedle
Street. It must cost the old girl a pretty penny to
keep it up, but she does it bravely. The object is to
afford the public the strongest possible protection
against fraud. Every note ever issued by the Bank has
its appropriate place in a book, and if it ever comes
back its record is marked out, and then it is dead.
No matter how well executed may be a counterfeit,
two of the same number cannot be redeemed without
the fraud being detected before the day is over.

The note itself is quite a costly piece of work, for
no expense is spared in its production. All the work,
except making the paper, is done upon the Bank's
premises. The best of materials are used in all the
branches. The paper is of wonderful tenacity, a sheet,
though so thin as to weigh only eighteen grains, being able to sustain fifty-six pounds weight. The
printing ink is made from the charred husks and seeds
and vines of Rhenish grapes, mixed with linseed oil,

and is of extraordinary intensity of blackness. The greater part of the lettering of the notes is printed from steel plates, but the numbering and cypher work is done on the ordinary printing press. I believe each note goes through the presses three or four times and between thirty and forty thousand are printed every day. The cost of producing all these paper promises, as I said before, cannot be a light matter, and it looks a little extravagant, therefore, to see them destroyed almost as soon as they are printed, which is the case with the bulk of them. A very stringent copyright protects these brief works of the Old Lady. To imitate one of her notes involved capital punishment until 1831, when the penalty was changed to transportation. The latter penalty is meted to the man who merely imitates the paper on which her bills are printed.

The nice old porter conducted us through an immense number of rooms, including the printing and bookbinding departments, and more others than I can now remember. The printing office was a pretty extensive concern, but the bookbindery was something astonishing. Between three and four hundred account books are ruled, printed and bound for the use of the Old Lady's clerks every week.

The business of the Bank is greatly increased by its agency for the British Government. The interest on the different classes of the national debt are paid here. There are at least a dozen separate offices for

this work, each more spacious than most of our largest banks, and employing a great many clerks.   On
"dividend day," I am told, the scene in these departments is one of extraordinary animation and activity,
and the amount of business which is done between
nine and five o'clock of such a day is almost incredible.
Confusion would be worse confounded if it were not
for the perfect system of doing the work.   Each room
has a large sign indicating the particular kind of bonds
which are there attended to, and the desks are let-
tered so as to show where to apply, according to the
name in which the bonds stand.   If I were fortunate
enough, we will say, to be one of England's creditors,
and wanted to get the interest of my money, being a
stranger I should very likely go to the wrong room,
if one of the army of porters on duty about the courts
did not point out the right one.   Once safely there,
even so stupid a fellow as this present writer could
hardly go to the wrong desk when the letter "M"
plainly stares him in the face from the right one.
The government securities are held in the names of
the owners, and certain days in every week are appointed for transfers of the stock.   Most of this business is done through brokers.   When a sale of stock
is made, buyer and seller, or their agents, go to the
Bank, and a clerk examines the register to see if the
seller actually owns the stock which he proposes to
transfer.   If all is correct the transfer is made out,
the parties sign the book, and the purchaser thence-

forth has "money in the funds" until he in turn parts with the right.

It was too late in the day for us to obtain admission to the bullion room, which I should have the more regretted if I had not, very shortly before I left America, been shut up in a little room in the Treasury Department at Washington, in which room there were about two hundred millions of symbolic dollars, a few millions of which I was permitted to have in possession a moment or two; and that was quite as much money and quite as good money as I cared about seeing. But our guide showed us all he could, and told us all he knew about what we saw, and was altogether such a clever old soul that I slipped a good reward into his hand, in spite of the injunction upon my ticket to the effect that "gratuities to the Company's servants are not permitted." I dare say he was grateful, but I am sure he was not surprised, (nobody about the Bank could be surprised by money, I think,) which led me to the conclusion that this rule of the Worshipful Company, like the rules of many other corporations, was a mere dead letter.

When we were out of the Bank I took a good look at its exterior, and having driven around it obtained an idea of its immense extent. It covers an area of about eight acres, but is a very singular-looking pile, having not a single outside window, the light being admitted to the various departments by nine open courts. There are nearly a thousand persons em-

8*

ployed within its walls, and the Company pays salaries and pensions to the amount of a quarter a million
of pounds sterling per annum.   The Old Lady takes
good care of her servants.   In whatever capacity they
labor, they receive increased pay according to the
length of time they have been in her service; and after
a certain number of years they can retire upon a pen-
sion equal to the highest salaries they have enjoyed.
It is said that not a few of them become so attached
to the service that they continue their work for years
after they might receive just as much money without
any labor at all, a fact that speaks well for both mistress and servants.   Many are the stories current il-
lustrating this devotion to the Old Lady.   A former
Chief Cashier was never known to ask a holiday but
once, and then only for a fortnight.   But he returned
after three days, satisfied that there was no recreation
worth taking, except in the service of his mistress.
Another old servant, on his death-bed, expressed the
wish to die on the steps of the Bank!

To jump from St. Paul's Cathedral and the Bank
of England down to a Wax-work show is to go from
the sublime to the ridiculous, I am sure my readers
will think, whose notions of wax-work are formed
from what they have seen in Barnum's Museum.   But
I can assure them that the comparison may be as
properly drawn between St. Paul's and an American
country church, or between the Bank of England and
an American country bank, as between Madame Tus-

saud's Wax-work Exhibition, of which I am about to
speak, and anything in that line ever displayed by
the great American showman. The establishment is
now in Portman Square, one of the most fashionable
parts of the city, and is fitted up in really elegant
style. In the different saloons there are more than
three hundred full-length figures of historical personages, attired as they appeared in life, and some of
them certainly remarkably correct likenesses. The
figures are arranged in groups, the principal ones, of
course, being composed of royal Courts. The gorgeous and costly robes worn on State occasions are here
faithfully reproduced, at an expense which must have
been enormous. The first room which attracts the
visitor's attention is a memorial or shrine in honor of
the Duke of Wellington, in which the departed hero
is represented as he looked when Lying in State,
surrounded by the emblems of the various honors
which had been heaped upon him. The likeness is
said to be perfect. Upon a wall of this room hangs
Sir G. Hayter's great picture of " Wellington visiting the Relics of Napoleon," the portrait in it being
the last the Duke sat for. This is a very fine painting, but only one of many valuable pictures which are
displayed in the rooms. In fact, the exhibition is
worth visiting as a Picture Gallery, quite independent
of the attractions offered by the wax-work models.
One room, called the Golden Chamber, is filled with
interesting relics of the Emperor Napoleon; among

others, the camp bedstead which he used during seven
years at St. Helena, with the mattrasses and pillow
on which he died. On the bed reposes a figure of
the exile in his Chasseur uniform and the cloak he
wore at Marengo. The likeness is from the original
cast from his face taken by his surgeon. Portraits
and busts of the various members of the Bonaparte
family are in this room, and the regalia and State
robes of the Court. In an adjoining room are placed
the Emperor's carriage captured at Waterloo, his
State carriage, and the one he used at St. Helena. It
would take more space than I can spare to mention
the curious relics of the great warrior which are gathered together in this room. There is another room,
called the "Chamber of Horrors," which is filled with
the figures of some of the worst criminals which this
wicked world has produced. Here, also, is a model
of the first Guillotine, and the identical Knife which
decapitated twenty-two thousand persons during the
first French Revolution, amongst whom were Louis
XVI., Marie Antoinette, the Duc de Orleans, and
most of the best blood of France, as well as Robe-
spierre, Carrier, and others among the worst. This
Knife is called "the most extraordinary relic in the
world," and was bought from the grandson of the
original executioner. I fear you will begin to think
that I am trying to write a "first-rate puff" of this
establishment, but you will be mistaken if you do, for
I have only intended to impress my opinion on the

reader, who may meditate a visit to London, that
Tussaud's Wax-work Exhibition is one of the most
interesting of London sights.

The greater part of a day ought to be spent in the
Zoological Gardens in Regent's Park, though I unfortunately had to " do " them in a few hours. I suppose it is the most complete collection in the world.
Certainly I have seen nothing like it. The Gardens
are very extensive and beautifully laid out, and would
be worth a visit if for nothing more than to see the
grounds and flowers. Everything is arranged in picturesque style — clumps of shrubby trees, patches of
flowers, miniature lakes, rustic cottages, green mea-
dows with little paddocks for the deer and other animals, great houses for the larger animals, and cages
of wire and glass as big as mansions where the birds
live apparently as much at home as in their native
woods. Neat gravel walks conduct the visitors to
the different departments, and one is pretty sure to
meet in his path a huge elephant carrying a castle
loaded with delighted children. The collection numbers nearly two thousand living specimens, more than
a hundred and fifty belonging to the mammalia alone,
among which are a pair of splendid hippopotami.
There are an immense number of monkeys, some so
big and human-looking that one expects to hear them
speak; but you need not infer, because I make special
mention of the monkeys, that I have a fellow feeling
for them. " On the contrary, quite the reverse." I

cannot catalogue the collection for you; let it suffice
to say that almost every known specimen which is
exhibited in any city is duplicated here.

I begin to find that I have gone too much into detail thus far in this letter, so that I have no room to
say a word about many other matters of which I
ought to tell you. I have spent much time in the
streets, which have a peculiar attraction for me.
One gets a better idea of London in walking about
the city than in any other way. You soon realize
something of its vastness. The never-ending din
and turmoil is spread over so vast a space that
it seems impossible to find an end to it. Yet there
are many green spots in the mighty wilderness of
houses, even at its very heart. Were it not for
the Parks many poor Londoners would never see a
foot of God's green earth. Oh! what misery, sin and
wretchedness confront the stranger at every turn!
I have seen more of squalid poverty here in two weeks
than in all my life before, and yet I have not been
into the lower portions of the city. Such dirty drabs
of ragged women at every corner, begging for money,
to be spent at the gin-palaces most likely! It is
common to suppose that beer is the favorite drink of
the lower classes of the English. Perhaps it is — in
the country. In London I should say that gin is the
ruling passion, certainly with the poor women. To
an American it looks very strange to see women
walking alone into these crowded Temples of Intem-

perance, at late hours of the night, and call for their drams of gin — some of them, too, not altogether without an air of respectability about them. At least, if all the women who drink gin in public houses at night in London are bad women, I wonder how the rising generation of Londoners can have any respect for their mothers. They are such quarrelsome wretches also. I have had occasion several times to take a " Hansom " in the evening a not long distance. I don't think there has been a time in which I have not passed a crowd gathered around some women screaming and fighting. Last night a scene of this kind occurred, which I observed from my window. It was past midnight. Hearing a woman's voice scolding and swearing, I looked out. Across the street, near a gin-palace, three women in black rags were standing. One was a tall, big creature, and she was the noisy one. She was using fearful language and threatening to " take the liver out " of a smaller woman, who seemed to be quietly mocking her. Suddenly the little woman darted at the big one like a tigress, tore off her bonnet, and would doubtless have " punished " her opponent dreadfully if a policeman had not come up at the moment and separated them. I supposed he would march them off to the station-house, but he did not. He started the big one off one way (she all the time loudly promising to " do for " the other at some future time), whilst the little woman and her companion quietly walked into the gin-shop, perhaps to celebrate the victory. I wondered why these women were not arrested, but a moment's reflection convinced me that the policemen must be instructed not to make arrests unless absolute mischief or injury is done; for if they did incarcerate all the fighting women there would have to be twice as many lock-ups as there are in London. I know you will think I might find a pleasanter topic than this to write about, but I must remind you that I write of matters which impress me most, without paying much regard to the fitness of things.

I do not in this letter so much as mention many notable places which I have visited, for it seems hardly worth while to say "I have been" here and there, or "I have seen" this and that, or "I have heard" so and so; and that would be all I should have room for now. Since my last I have made a trip to a certain old town about a hundred miles from here — a dull sleepy little place in Suffolk, which has not an object worth the tourist's attention, never produced a celebrated man, and the only incident in whose history that has been thought worthy of record is the fact that Queen Elizabeth passed through it in one of her state progresses — yet an old town that I was more anxious to visit than any other place in Europe. You will guess the reason why. Nothing was changed, hardly, since I saw it twenty-one years ago, and yet how different everything looked from what I expected! Can that little stream be the

river of which I used to be so proud? Are those
dingy little holes the splendid shops which used to
display such treasures in their windows? Did I
ever think it a great feat to "buck" over those low
posts? Such and such-like questions I was continually asking myself. But it was not all disappointment
either. There were some pleasures for me in that old
town worth the journey across the Atlantic to procure. — — But this cannot interest more than a very
few of my readers, yet I am sure the rest will pardon
the digression.

I must close this letter, but not until I have told
you that Dr. W. and his party arrived to-day from
Paris, and are stopping at the same hotel with me.
Many of your readers will be glad to hear they are
all well. Good-bye.

XI.

SOMETHING MORE ABOUT THE SIGHTS OF LONDON. — THE
PALACE OF SYDENHAM, AND A GRAND CONCERT THEREIN.
— A TRIP TO RICHMOND, AND A DINNER AT THE STAR
AND GARTER. — A RAMBLE IN KEW GARDENS. — VISITS
TO LAMBETH PALACE, AND "THE TIMES" OFFICE. — A
DAY AT WINDSOR. — WESTMINSTER ABBEY. — AN ENIGMA
SOLVED. — FAREWELL TO LONDON.

PORTSMOUTH, Sept. 6th, 1866.

I did not intend to let the last steamer sail without
carrying you a letter from me, but the fates were
against me. I could not find time to write the last
week in London, a fact which will not, I am sure,
astonish any of my readers who know the place.
There are so many "sights" you feel reluctant to go
away without seeing — so many things which *must*
be done whether you see anything or not — that the
time left for writing must be taken out of the night,
and it is a chance whether you do not find such work
a physical impossibility after the fatigues of the day.
At any rate that was my experience, and the consequence is that I must depend upon my memory more

than I usually do for what I shall now write touching our adventures since the date of my last letter.
And when I say " our adventures " please understand
that I now include five persons, the friends of whom I
spoke recently having returned from Paris and joined
my little party — intending, also, to sail with us for
home.

In my first letter from London I spoke of a day
spent at the Sydenham Crystal Palace, and said we
would endeavor to go there again, having only seen
sufficient on that occasion to convince us that, in comparison of what there was to be seen in the Palace,
we had seen nothing. We did spend another day at
that bewildering place, and the result was as before
— we wanted to go again. It was something of a sacrifice to go the second time, when we took into consideration the number of places we should not be able
to visit at all, so few were the days left to us in the
great metropolis if we sailed for America on the day
appointed according to our original plan; but even
when we had studied the list we had drawn up of
places which every stranger ought to visit, and found
that more than two-thirds of them were impossible
pleasures for us, we still decided that we would rather
pay a second visit to the Crystal Palace than a first
to any of the other " sights " of London.

I speak of the Sydenham Palace as one of the sights
of London. Properly speaking, of course it is not,
Sydenham being between seven and eight miles from

the city; but so many trains run there every day, and the fare is such a trifle, that the Palace is far easier and less expensive to reach than many localities within the modern Babylon.   Besides, there is no one place where so many Londoners can be seen at one time; so it is fair enough to speak of it as one of the many sights of which London can boast.   The managers of the Palace advertise it as "the most wonderful shilling's worth of amusement in the world," and so it is, and so it would be if there was nothing but the Palace, its contents, and the grounds to see. But there are some very attractive performances given there every day, the principal feature offered this season having been a series of ballad concerts by the best artists to be had in London.   You will not wonder that, after we had examined the programme for the "Last of the Season," and found that Sims Reeves, Madame Parepa, Miss Edmonds, Madame Rudersdorff and Mr. Weiss were to sing, that Mr. Levy was to play some of his surprising cornet solos, and that the famous band of the Coldstream Guards was to be in the orchestra — you will not wonder, I say, after reading this list of attractions, that we came to the conclusion that we could not possibly choose a better day for our second visit.   I had a greater desire to hear Sims Reeves than any other singer whom I never had heard, having read much of the wonderful ability and hardly less remarkable eccentricity of the great English tenor.   I frankly confess, also, that

I expected to be disappointed in him; but, having heard him, I must as frankly admit that in my opinion he deserves his high reputation.

However, this is not the orthodox method of dishing up a day's sight-seeing: I ought to begin at the beginning, as is my usual custom — and a tedious custom it is, I am frequently reminded. If I do follow that plan now I must tell you that the trip to Sydenham is well worth taking, if only to see what an enormously expensive piece of railway you travel over, if you take the route known as the "High Level." This is one continued mass of bridge and masonry work, almost the whole distance, being built above the level of the houses for the most part. I think there are nearly a dozen stopping places in less than eight miles, and if London keeps on growing as rapidly as it does at present, there is very little doubt that in a few years Sydenham will in reality be a part of the great city.

After we arrived at the Palace we spent a good deal of our spare time in the Picture Gallery, which is really one of the most attractive as well as one of the most useful features of the enterprise. There are more than twelve hundred paintings exhibited, the greater part being the works of modern British artists, with a good sprinkling of foreign pictures, and a few valuable works of the old masters. The superb copies of the celebrated Cartoons of Raphael, at Hampton Court, which were painted by Antonio

Verrio, by order of William the Third, are there, and (I mention the fact for the benefit of our Academy of Fine Arts) these seven paintings are waiting for a purchaser—but I did not enquire the price. Indeed, nearly all the pictures are for sale, the price being plainly attached to each, a plan which adds much to the interest of the exhibition. One likes to know the value which is placed upon a picture, whether he wants to buy it or not; and if he does decide to purchase, he is quite certain of getting his picture at the artists' price. The paintings are sent in by artists, with the price they hold them at. The Company rejects all such as possess no merit, nor do they allow any copies to be exhibited. I have seen no better place to select modern pictures from. American gentlemen who are forming Galleries would do well to examine this collection. I noticed a good many really beautiful works which would be snapped up quickly in our town at a good advance above the prices marked—a hint for dealers. For myself, I was strongly—very strongly—tempted to spend money that I could not afford. You, who know me, will understand what a trial this was, and you can "fancy my feelings" quite correctly, I am sure.

After looking at the pictures there was but little time left before the concert commenced, but we improved it in wandering about the long aisles and galleries of the wonderful Palace. At every step we saw something to admire—something we had not noticed on our first visit; or, if we had, we found we had not looked at it half enough. What a grand scene that was which we enjoyed from the centre of the Nave, where the best general view of the interior of the Palace can be obtained! Near us was a magnificent crystal fountain standing in a sheet of water bordered with rich flowers. At each end of this fairy lake the gigantic leaves of the *Victoria Regia* were floating, and the intermediate space was filled with various other aquatic plants, rare and beautiful. The airy arches of the lofty roof were mirrored in the clear water, wherever its glittering surface was free from the dark green leaves of the plants. Great trees and shrubs and plants of almost every clime were growing on either side of the Nave, setting off with perfect harmony the pure white of the marble statues which were interspersed in the scene.

But we could not linger on this enchanted ground more than a few minutes, for we wanted to take a peep into the numerous Courts which form so interesting and instructive a feature in the arrangement of the building. The object of these Courts is to present "specimens of the various phases through which the arts of Architecture and Sculpture have passed, commencing from the earliest known period, and coming down to modern times — a period of more than three thousand years." To carry out this idea great spaces of the Palace are built and fitted up into different Courts, standing in which the visitor may imagine himself transported as if by magic to other lands in other ages. So immense is the extent of the Palace that room is afforded for the perfect development of this plan. There is an Egyptian Court, a Greek Court, a Roman Court, an Alhambra Court, an Assyrian Court, a Byzantine and Romanesque Court, a German Mediæval Court, an English Mediæval Court, a Pompeian Court, and various Vestibules, each large enough to look like the original, and each, both in exterior and interior decorations, a correct representation of the style imitated. A moderate-sized volume would hardly contain a description of the contents of these Courts alone. They are filled with specimens of the Arts of the different periods and countries.

We could not even give a look at the thousand-and-one other attractions of the Palace, and we found ourselves very soon discussing the possibility of giving a third day to the work, when, by coming very early, staying very late, and improving every fleeting moment of the time, we might perchance manage to bring away an intelligible idea of what there was to be seen. The Palace is of such immense extent that a mere walk through its many aisles and galleries is no light undertaking. A week could be spent in admiring the marvellous structure, and the beautiful grounds belonging to it; and if I had the time to spare I would give the week to the work. But I must not prose about the wonders of the Palace any longer, or I shall be too late for the concert, and I would not like to miss any of the entertainment. The concerts are given in the centre transept, a vast space being fitted up for the purpose. I wondered how it could be possible to hear the singers, supposing their voices would be lost in that immense building, but soon discovered that there was no difficulty about it, at least not where our seats were. There were at least ten thousand people present, I should think, fully one-fourth of the number having taken seats at half-a-crown, or at a shilling, extra; for, you must know, that though a shilling admits you to the Palace, and to the concert, there are no seats provided except for the above additional prices; so it is not so very cheap a concert, after all, if you want a good place. I gave you the names of the performers, in the beginning, and you will be prepared to believe that the entertainment was a fine one; but I think it will astonish some of your readers who have heard Madame Parepa, to learn that Sims Reeves was a greater attraction, was more loudly applauded, and more persistently encored, than that glorious singer. He sang "The Maid of Llangollen," "When other Lips," and the "Death of Nelson." I was not much surprised — perhaps even a little disappointed — at the first and second, for though his voice was beautifully pure and sweet, and his execution perfect, he had not as much power as I had expected; but I never heard a song so well sung, with such wonder-

9

ful expression and with such an amazing effect, as his
last song. The great audience was excited to the
wildest enthusiasm, waved hats aud handkerchiefs,
and demanded a repetition with an emphasis that was
not to be denied. The singer tried to be let off with
bowing his acknowledgment of the compliment. He
had succeeded in this when recalled after his other
songs, but it would not do now: the applause and
cheering were growing almost frantic, when he came
out the second time and repeated the last verse. Of
course some of this enthusiasm was due to the sentiment of the piece, but yet no one could deny that the
applause was well deserved. Sims Reeves must be
nearly fifty years old. He is a rather small man, with
short black curly hair and a black — too black —
moustache. His face is deeply lined, the tracings
being, I fear, not entirely the work of age. If he
ever sung better than he does now, which would seem
to be almost certain considering his years and his not
altogether abstemious habits, he must have been a
glorious tenor indeed. He treats his audiences very
cavalierly, it is said, and the chances are considered
about even that he will disappoint them when he is
expected to appear. He has occasioned more mana-
gerial apologies than any artist living, and sometimes
gets awfully "wigged" by the public in consequence.
But they say that hisses inspire him — that he sings
his best always just after he has behaved his worst,
and that no audience can be ill-tempered with him

when he does sing his best. All of which I am prepared to believe, now that I have heard him sing
" The Death of Nelson."

After having said so much about Mr. Reeves, you
will certainly think me ungallant if I do not say at
least as much of the female performers, but I can't
help that — I have not the time, nor can you spare
me the room. Besides, you all know the magnificent
Parepa — I could not speak any higher praise of her
than she has already received with you. She sang
three ballads, and was each time encored. Madame
Rudersdorff is a fine-looking woman, with an extremely powerful soprano voice; but I imagine that
her best days as a singer passed some years ago.
Miss Edmonds is a very pretty singer, and must appear to great advantage in a concert room. Mr.
Weiss is not likely to set the Thames on fire, though
he is considered a first-rate artist, I believe. You
have not forgotten the tremendous strains which *the*
Levy blew from that cornet. He blew harder than
ever this time, as though he would fill that vast space
with sound. He appears to be very popular. Take
it for all in all, it was a great concert, well worth the
money it cost to hear it, including the extra half-
crowns for seats.

You have heard of Richmond Hill, and of the famous " Star and Garter " tavern. We spent a day in
visiting that delightful place, taking a lovely day (oh,
rare event !) for it, and doing the journey — about

ten miles — by carriage. I suppose there is no prettier spot in England than Richmond, and the view
from the window of the great coffee room of the Star
and Garter, just upon the brow of the hill, is one not
to be forgotten. The beautiful valley of the Thames
is seen for a long distance, the silvery stream gleam-
ing in the sunlight as it winds its tortuous way to the
sea. Everybody makes a point of going to Richmond,
and everybody is right. I suppose they nearly all
dine at least once at the Star and Garter, too, and
perhaps a second time — if they have any money left.
You can certainly get a splendid dinner there, but
you will just as certainly have to pay a splendid price
for it. The greatest state is observed in the service.
The head man in the coffee room looks as though he
might be Grand Butler to the Queen, and the waiters
are very solemnly polite. Perhaps there is just a little too much ceremony for comfort. The unsophisti-
cated guest is apt to be a little over-awed by it, and,
consequently, to become nervous and awkward, as
was the case with a certain friend of mine, a not generally bashful gentleman, who dropped a potato on
the floor whilst we were dining. That unfortunate
man was seated at the same table with me — was in
the same party in fact. At home he is not given to
such practices — was never accused of nervous mod-
esty in all his life. Shall I ever forget the cold chill
of horror which ran through me when the miserable
potato dodged his fork and jumped upon the floor,

spitefully rolling into a conspicuous place where it was the observed of all observers? Of course the solemn humbug of a waiter did not fail to make the most of the situation. I see him now, spreading a large napkin over the obnoxious vegetable and carefully lifting it, as though it was the hottest potato that ever was cooked! "Do men travel three or four thousand miles away from home to drop potatoes at the dinner table?" I sternly demanded of the guilty wretch who brought down ridicule upon us. I rejoiced, and glory in the confession though I was myself a fellow-sufferer, when I saw what a snug little sum the feast had cost him.

Whatever effect this incident may have had upon my appetite, it did not quite spoil our enjoyment of the drive through the magnificent Park, one of the finest in England, nearly nine miles in circumference. The extensive grounds of this splendid domain present a variety of scenery which is enchanting to the eye. Some of the noblest trees I ever saw are there, and the gently-rising slopes are alive with deer. The Park belongs to the Crown, but has for many generations been freely open to the public; in fact it may now be said to belong to the public. Charles the First enclosed it with a brick wall, an offence which was one of the counts in his indictment. In the reign of George the Third an attempt was made to exclude the public, but a brewer named Lewis contested the case with the Crown and established a right of way.

Since then the privileges of the people have not been interfered with.

We had driven before dinner about the village, and admired the prospect from the summit of Richmond Hill. I don't like to copy another man's description of this view, especially as my own poor words will appear still more thread-bare by comparison — but yet I want to give you the best idea I can of what we saw, and this is right to my hand:

"Of all that belongs to the beautiful in scenery nothing here is wanting. Wood and water, softly swelling hills and hazy distance, with village spires and lordly halls, are blended in beautiful harmony. From the gentle slope of the hill a vast expanse of country stretches far away, 'till the distance is closed by the hills of Buckinghamshire on the north-west, and the Surrey Downs on the south-east, and all this intermediate space is one wide valley of the most luxuriant fertility; but appearing to the eye a succession of densely wooded tracts, broken and diversified by a few undulations of barren uplands, and here and there a line of white vapory smoke, with a tower or spire marking the site of a goodly town or humble village. In the midst the broad placid river, studded with islets and its surface alive with flocks of swans and innumerable pleasure skiffs, winds gracefully away 'till lost among the foliage, only to be occasionally tracked afterward by a glittering thread of silver seen as the sun glances suddenly upon it between the dark trunks of the trees; and something of majesty is added to the exceeding loveliness by Windsor's royal towers which loom out finely on the distant horizon."

On the way to Richmond we had stopped for an hour or so at the Kew Gardens, one of the most famous sights of London, but, like many of its other

attractions, some considerable distance from the city.
The Gardens are not very extensive, but they are most
beautifully laid out, and the grounds are kept in admirable order. The collection of plants from all parts
of the world is a rare one, and all have been arranged
and labeled by Sir William Hooker. Numerous flower
beds, conservatories and hot-houses invite attention.
Some of the glass houses look like miniature Crystal
Palaces, but only in miniature when compared with
that enormous building. One, called the great Palm
House, is sixty feet high, and was constructed at a
cost of nearly two hundred thousand dollars. This is
filled with the choicest exotics. Among the most attractive of the plants are the Egyptian Papyrus, the
Bread-fruit tree, the Cow tree, the Cocoa-nut, Coffee,
Banana, and a beautiful Weeping Willow, reared from
a slip taken from the tree which shaded Napoleon's
grave at St. Helena. There is an enclosed Conserva-
tory or winter garden, more than twice as large as the
Palm House; a Museum in which every variety of
wood, in planks and blocks, are exhibited; and a
Temperate House two hundred and twelve feet long,
one hundred and thirty-seven wide, and sixty high,
with two wings one hundred and twelve feet by sixty-
two. A pretty little lake has lately been constructed,
having communication with the Thames by a tunnel
under the river terrace. This beautiful place is maintained at the public expense, and improvements are
being constantly made. It was hard to be content

with the brief visit we could only give, but we made the best of it.

I am told that it is not an easy matter to obtain admittance to Lambeth Palace, the town residence of the Archbishops of Canterbury, and I must therefore record my thanks to the kind friend (Dr. W.) whose courtesy procured us this pleasure. It is a curious and venerable structure, exhibiting various styles of architecture, many Archbishops having added to the original building during the six centuries that it has been the archiepiscopal residence. The Chapel, in which the Archbishops are always consecrated, and where the first American Bishop was consecrated, is six hundred years old. At its western end is a tower, called the Lollard's Tower, from some Lollards or Wickliffites having been imprisoned there. We climbed up into a little room at the top of this tower which appeared to have been the actual place of confinement. Strong iron rings were in the walls, and many names of the prisoners, with pious ejaculations and broken sentences, were cut in the thick oak wainscotting. One of these inscriptions, considering the solitude of the unfortunate prisoner, appeals strongly to the sympathies of the beholder: "*Jhs cyppe me out of alle el compane, Amen.*" (Jesus, keep me out of all evil company.)

We were conducted through all but the private apartments of the Palace, one of which, it was whispered to us, was occupied by a little stranger, not entirely unconnected with an interesting event announced a few days previous in The Times. I wonder if Archbishops are as pleased and proud as other grandfathers proverbially are? This is a digression, however. I must go back, and speak of the great library, founded by Archbishop Bancroft, who died in 1610, and now containing twenty-five thousand volumes, many of them scarce works of ancient date, with a goodly list of rare old books of divinity. The great hall of the Palace is hung with the portraits of all the Archbishops. Lambeth is not considered a healthy part of the town, but the Palace is a very stately residence. It is fit, indeed, that it should be, for is not the Archbishop of Canterbury Primate of all England and first subject of the Crown, taking rank next after the royal family? Back of the Palace are extensive gardens (about thirty acres) beautifully laid out, and, as seen from the river, with the tall old trees in the back ground, adding much to the picturesque effect of the building.

I could not expect to astonish you with an account of our visit to the office of The Times, though there was one circumstance connected with it which astonished us all, viz: it was the only place any of the party had yet visited in England, where a fee to the person who showed us about was absolutely refused; a circumstance, you may be sure, in which I took no little professional pride. Being Saturday, it was not the best day to see the operations of the great news-

9*

paper, but yet we saw enough to admire and wonder at.   There is not so much difference, however, in the workings of this concern and the first-class papers of America, as I had expected to find.   I cannot help the belief that much of the importance with which the "Thunderer" is invested is due to the extreme discipline which is maintained in the office, and the mystery which its conductor insists upon in regard to the writers for its columns.   No one about the office is allowed to give the address of any of the contributors or regular writers; an absurd rule, one would think, when the fact can be so readily obtained by other means.   The circulation of The Times is not so large as that of several of the New York dailies, and it has at least three competitors in London who outrank it in this respect.   The Telegraph claims to have the largest circulation of any daily paper in the world; The Star, I believe, comes next, and The Standard advertises itself as "the *largest* newspaper in the world."   The price of The Times being three times as much as its competitors charge, and the difference in quality being after all more a tradition than anything else, it is not to be wondered at that the great Jove of the Press does not so completely eclipse its cotemporaries as it formerly did.   The other three papers I have named advertise very extensively—they all have huge posters in the railway stations and wherever such announcements are allowed.   In fact, they appear to have the greatest faith in the system

by which they live (for I imagine that not only all
their profits, but most of their working expenses,
also, must be derived from advertising, so small is
the sum for which they are sold), and they set very
stimulating examples to their customers in this respect. The Star's great card is the "Readings by
Starlight," a series of papers contributed by Mr.
James Greenwood, author of the remarkable sketch
"A Night in a Workhouse, by an Amateur Casual,"
which excited such an extraordinary sensation throughout England some months ago, a sensation that has
not entirely subsided yet. The experience narrated,
as you doubtless remember, was an actual one, the
enterprising writer having disguised himself and secured admittance as a casual pauper. The horrible
adventure was so graphically described that it produced the effect of a faithful photograph. It brought
the author money and fame, placing him at one step
in the front rank of sketch-writers; but I doubt
whether he would repeat the experiment for double
the reward, though a host of imitators did spring up
like mushrooms, filling the newspapers with "Nights"
in all sorts of dreadful places.

I could not leave London without paying a visit to
Windsor, much as I was pressed for time, and therefore gave up most of my last day to that excursion.
I shall not be able, however, to give you much of an
idea of what we saw; owing, first, to the hurried way
in which we "did" the place, and, second, to the still

greater hurry in which I am at the present writing.
The day was not a pleasant one, and we were obliged
to limit ourselves to an inspection of the Castle and
Chapel, and a very brief drive in the Park. Luckily,
the appearance of the Castle is as familiar to most
readers as to myself, and I can therefore spare you,
and be spared myself, any attempt at description.
But I must not fail to observe that the stately and
venerable seat of British royalty more than realized
my expectations. There is something about it to inspire the awe with which one contemplates a magnificent Cathedral, as well as the admiration due to any
noble specimen of architecture. William the Conqueror was the founder of the Castle, though it was
nearly entirely rebuilt during the reign of Edward the
Third, under the charge of the celebrated William
of Wykeham, who was so proud of his work that he
caused this inscription to be cut in stone on one of the
towers: *"Hoc fecit Wykeham."* The words can be
read to this day. Tradition has it that the King was
exceeding wroth at the assumption of Wykeham, and
was only appeased by the latter's explanation that the
true reading of the inscription was, "the Tower made
Wykeham," and not "Wykeham made the Tower,"
as the King had supposed. I hope the fraud was not
recorded against the pious Bishop. For nearly eight
centuries the Castle has been the principal residence
of England's monarchs, and has grown into greater
favor than ever with the latter sovereigns. Victoria

makes it her usual winter residence. During her absence admission is readily obtained to the Castle.
We were conducted through the State Apartments,
which did not strike us as being at all magnificent,
compared with what we had seen in Palaces on the
Continent, though in better taste than many of them,
and not too splendid for service. If you would know
more of what we saw in the Audience Chamber, which
is hung with Gobelins tapestry; of the Presence
Chamber, which is decorated in the Louis Quatorze
style; of the Vandyke Room, so called because its
walls are hung with twenty-two works by that master; of the Guard Chamber, where the walls are decorated with arms, and which contains many interesting
relics connected with England's victories, the most
notable of them being a part of the foremast of Nelson's flag-ship, the *Victory*, with a colossal bust of the
hero upon it; of St. George's Hall, containing portraits of the latter British sovereigns; of the grand
Waterloo Gallery, which is ornamented with the
"counterfeit presentments" of the most eminent soldiers and statesmen connected with that famous battle; of many other apartments which are freely opened
to the public (though the polite attendant who con-
ducts you will not disdain the gratuity you slip into
his hand in spite of the "commands of Her Majesty"
to the contrary); if, I say, you would know more of
these things than I have now told you, are not they
written in a little Guide-Book which can be bought
for a shilling?

The business of the village is mainly derived from visitors to the Castle. The privilege of inspection is only granted when the Queen is absent; but Her Majesty resides so much at the Castle that there are not nearly as many visitors as formerly, and the citizens consequently complain of dull times, not forgetting to lay the blame upon the Queen, who is certainly not at all popular in Windsor. In fact, I fear that Victoria is fast becoming very obnoxious to all classes of her subjects. She is obstinate and ill-tempered, it is said, and I grieve to add that very ugly stories are freely told about her habits. I hope they are not true, but it certainly must strike every one who has seen her later photographic portraits that her face is an exceedingly unamiable one. Many people profess to think that she will resign the Crown if she lives many years longer; and there is but little doubt that public opinion will exert a powerful pressure toward that result, if the half of what bad things are told about her should come to be generally believed.

But I am wandering from my text again, and that, too, when I have very little space left for such exercise. I must get back to London as quickly as possible, for this letter will be my last about that city. Stop a few minutes first, though, to look through that noble example of Gothic architecture, St. George's Chapel, which is a part of Windsor Castle. The interior of the Chapel is surpassingly beautiful, the roof of the Choir, in particular, being a most remarkable piece of work. It was executed in 1508, by Sir Reginald Bray, at the expense of the Knights of the Garter. The interior of the Choir is decorated with the richest wood carvings I have ever seen. Within, above the stalls, are suspended the banners, mantles, swords and helmets of all the Knights of the Garter, and therein the ceremony of installation takes place. The Choir window is a memorial to the late Prince Albert, and was executed at the expense of the Dean and Canons of Windsor. It is an admirable piece of work, having many sections representing in beautifully stained glass a number of scriptural subjects. The base of the window has fourteen small sections depicting as many different scenes in the life of the Prince Consort. Annexed to it are the armorial bearings of the Prince, and a Latin inscription of which the following is a translation : " *To the Honor of God and to the Memory of the most regretted Prince, the Dean and Canons, deeply mourning, have dedicated this window.*"

St. George's Chapel contains a great number of interesting monuments, and the tombs of all the present dynasty and many of their ancestors. Few of the monuments possess any great merit as works of art. The best of all — and that, indeed, is a very beautiful work — is the cenotaph to the memory of Princess Charlotte, the lamented daughter of George the Fourth. It was executed by Wyatt, at a cost of one hundred and fifty thousand dollars, collected by voluntary contributions. The Princess, you know, was the idol and hope of the nation. Any description I could give would fail to convey an idea of the composition, which is somewhat singular but very poetical and beautiful, and I will not therefore attempt it.

As I approach the close of this letter I am conscious of how very little I have told you about London — or even about what I have seen of that metropolis of the world; for, compared with what there is to see, I have seen almost nothing. I meant to do better, but could not possibly steal the time necessary to do justice to my work. You must take the will for the deed. Do not think that what I have spoken of is a tithe of what I could speak, were I to only name the things I was most impressed with. And don't think, especially, because I have not hitherto mentioned it, that I failed to visit Westminster Abbey, though I must own that my stay there was necessarily so brief as to be hardly worth mentioning. That venerable sanctuary was the last place toward which I bent my steps before leaving London, and it was a satisfaction at least, if a poor one, to know that I did enter it, though that was almost all I could do.

Just here I am reminded that in a former letter I spoke of being puzzled by the street cries of London. One especially, which I had heard every morning, I promised to discover the meaning of, and reveal the mystery to you. I attributed it to an old fellow who shuffled past my window regularly at a certain hour with a bundle of papers under his arm. The cry, as near as I can render it, was "Stur–ur–ur!" After a good deal of speculation about the matter I came to the conclusion that the old man was a news boy — with copies of "The Star" for sale. Having settled the question satisfactorily, in my own mind, I was almost indignant one morning when an old woman was pointed out to me as the true author of the cry. I knew better! It *must* be the old man — and he was crying the "Star–ar–ar!" In my firm way (sometimes ignorantly styled an obstinate way — but that's no matter), I demanded absolute proof before I could be convinced that I was mistaken. I was dared to go into the street next morning and investigate for myself. I did go into the street, etc. And the result was — *not* as I had expected. I had to admit (but, then, you know, nobody is more ready to admit he is in the wrong than I am — *when* convinced of it) that the cry was uttered by the old woman. But what do you suppose she had to sell? You could never guess. *Water-cresses!*

I pondered a good deal over this matter of street-cries, trying to find a reason for their being so totally without meaning to a stranger, and at last arrived at this solution of the enigma:—the criers, I thought, must have regular beaten routes, and, consequently, almost as regular a set of customers ; so they have only to utter some regular cry — no matter what — and it will be recognized at once by the residents of the neighborhood, who, of course, know what they have to sell and only want to be notified of the right time to go to the door.

From London we came to Portsmouth (where I mail this letter), on the way to Ireland, intending to take the steamer at Queenstown, on the twentieth instant, for home. The two weeks intervening will be spent in hurried visits to the most interesting points we can stop at in England and Ireland in that brief period. I will try and write one more letter to you, just to make a round dozen of them.

I was about to say "Good night," but find that "Good morning" would be more strictly correct. You see what hard work I make of it — this writing about a holiday summer's trip. Well, I have seen the folly of it, and I can promise that if I am ever lucky enough to have another such holiday, I will not spoil it by inditing long epistles to anybody. "Good morning."

XII.

DUBLIN, September 13th, 1866.

Having determined that this shall be the last of my letters from Europe, I take up my pen (there's a nice old-fashioned expression for you!) with greater alacrity than usual, and in the hope that not many days after you receive the letter, the writer will be with you *in propriâ personâ*, as he has been in the spirit during the whole time of his absence. The thought of returning home again has all along been the pleasantest anticipation connected with my summer's holiday, a fact I have found it difficult to make some people believe, both in Europe and before I left America. But it is a fact, nevertheless, and I am sure you will not doubt it now that I repeat it here.

Home is home, after all, and there is no place like it,
as the dear old song says; but it is sometimes difficult for a man to determine *where* his home is, a
doubt which will never arise in my mind again, now
that I have tried a short absence from Buffalo.

But I must not waste any space in disquisitions on
a text foreign to my subject, and of no interest except to a very few of the nearest and dearest of my
friends, with whom I cannot appropriately converse
in the columns of a newspaper; especially as I shall
have more travel to note, and more sights to try and
describe in this than in any of my previous letters.

In my last I barely spoke of having arrived in
Portsmouth; now I will try and tell you something
of what we saw and did in our three days' stay in
that place.   Portsmouth is chiefly renowned as being
one of the greatest naval stations of England, and we
naturally spent a good deal of time in visiting its
dockyard.   Many of the finest Iron-clads in the British navy are stationed there, and we were fortunate
enough to have the company of a professional gentleman, thoroughly competent to describe them, when
we paid our visit.   You have not failed to notice the
tremendous outcry which John Bull is just now rais-
ing about the mismanagement of his naval affairs, and
I think that anybody who should see what we saw in
Portsmouth would admit that the old gentleman is
justified in his loud grumbling.   Magnificent vessels,
ruined by experiments to gratify the whims or pre-

judices of Admiralty Lords innocent of the faintest
practical knowledge of seamanship, lay in those docks
" thick as leaves in Vallambrosia," expensive monuments of a nation's folly in permitting a system to
exist so long after its total failure to meet the exigen-
cies of the time has been over and over again demonstrated. The only consolation which practical Eng-
lishmen appear to derive from this state of things is
that other nations have profited by England's expenditures. They claim that the experiments have been
in some degree necessary to develop the new system
of naval warfare inaugurated by the *Merrimac* and
Monitor in our rebellion. A very poor consolation
this must be, I should think, considering that on her
own supremacy on the seas depends England's position among the great powers of the world.

It must not be supposed from the above observations that we saw no ships in Portsmouth fit to con-
tend for the world's championship. England has
succeeded in producing several of the finest Iron-clads
afloat, the best specimen which we saw being the
Minatour, and a very noble ship she is. Her dimensions are enormous, and it is hard to say in what respect she could be improved, unless the whole idea of
her construction is wrong. She does not certainly
stand nearly so high out of the water as the old-fashioned three-deckers, but yet she presents a much
larger target to the enemies' guns than our own ships
do. Properly speaking, she is not an iron-clad, but

rather an iron ship wooden lined, her whole frame
being of heavy iron plate backed by an enormous
thickness of solid wood. If she succeeds in attaining
the speed which is expected, she would surely prove
an ugly customer, and there seems to be no doubt
whatever as to her sea-going qualities. In reference
to this ship the great complaint of the nation is that
she is not ready for sea, the time having long passed
when she ought to have been commissioned for active
duty; and this fault is not likely to be remedied in
less than six months at the very least. In fact, the
British Admiralty Board appears to make a point of
not getting any vessel out until new improvements
have demonstrated her utter unfitness for service
without a total change in the original plan of construction.

The dockyards of Portsmouth are very extensive,
but the government intends to increase their capacity
nearly double. The projected improvements were
explained to us, but I cannot conscientiously aver
that we understood them. Then we were shown
through the Arsenal and Gun-wharves, where we took
note of more big cannon and shot and shell than we
ever saw before. Having seen thus much, there was
little else to attract attention in Portsmouth, so we
took one day out of the three we intended for that
place for a trip over to the Isle of Wight — a trip
that we did not regret, you may be sure. The weather
was not propitious — quite the contrary, indeed, for it

blew great guns, and rained hard and steady most of
the day. I do not like to find fault, as you know,
and have been specially inclined to be pleased with
everything English, even to the weather; but the last
week's experience constrains me to admit that the cli-
mate is a trifle moist — or, not to put too fine a point
upon it, a little too " demnition wet," as Mr. Mantil-
ini would observe. We braved the storm, however,
on the day I speak of, and crossed over to Ryde in a
little steamer, where we took a carriage and drove to
Cowes, Osborne, Newport and Carisbrook, passing
on the way more pretty places, and stopping to admire
more beautiful scenery, than we had observed in any
one day before.

The Isle of Wight is one of the most charming bits
of God's earth. I remembered well how fresh and
green and inviting it looked that morning when I saw
it three months before, after ten days of looking out
upon the sea with no land in sight; and I had not forgotten how reluctant I was to pass the lovely island
without setting foot upon its shore. The villainous
weather could not quite spoil the zest with which I
enjoyed this day's excursion — a treat I had silently
promised myself that morning. My only regret was
that I could not now spare time to thoroughly explore
the island, in spite of wind and weather. The little
we did see was worth more than the trouble it cost.
So it would have been, indeed, if we could only have
seen Ryde, where we landed, which is a beautiful town

of nearly ten thousand inhabitants, and quite a fashionable summer resort, I imagine, from the number of
pleasure yachts we saw anchored there.   It is surrounded by pleasant groves and villas, lodges and
cottages, even the most modest-looking of which have
some distinguished title.   Everybody's local habita-
tion has a name in England, but I thought the rule
extended to the Nobodies as well, in Ryde, for there
is hardly a little eight-roomed house in the place but
it is blessed with an aristocratic-sounding title.

Some idea of the antiquity of Ryde may be gained
if I mention that a church in the neighborhood is said
to occupy the site upon which the first church in the
island was erected nearly twelve centuries ago.   The
place, however, though so old a settlement has only
recently began to grow.   For hundreds of years it
was a mere fishing village.   But fashion has taken
notice of it, and it is now a very thriving town.   In
the season I believe it is the rendezvous of the Royal
Yacht Club.   The pier is about half-a-mile long, built
into the sea, and on it we took our first ride on an
English tramway, one of those inventions of ours
being laid from the steamer's landing place to the
principal street of the town.

What little we saw of Osborne House, the delightful summer residence of the Queen, made us wish to
see more.   It is a very noticeable object from the sea
and looks all the more charming at first sight to the
tourist who has just crossed the stormy Atlantic, be-

cause he has been so longing for the sight of land. A
more romantic spot could not be imagined. Many of
Victoria's happiest hours have been spent there, for
it was a favorite residence with Prince Albert, who
took great pleasure in looking after his model farm
on the estate. Our drive took us through East and
West Cowes; showed us a little of Newport, the
capital of the Island, and its most ancient town; and
of the picturesque village of Carisbrook with its
ruined castle, the romantic aspect of which invited a
closer inspection than time or weather would permit
us to give. Nor did we fail to find some excitement
in the stormy passage back to Portsmouth, feeling no
little gratification in learning from an old salt that it
was "very nasty weather indeed,"—nasty enough
certainly to make us glad to reach port again.

From Portsmouth we took the rail to Leamington,
a rather too long trip, and carrying us past many
places where the tourist ought to linger. Winchester
was one of these; but I was more reluctant still to
pass renowned old Oxford, whose towers and spires
were aggravatingly visible a long distance. But such
was the haste in which our party was forced to travel,
and so much more anxious were we to spend the time
at Leamington, where we would be within a few miles
of Stratford, Kenilworth, Warwick Castle, and other
famous places, to visit which we made the route especially, that we hurried along regardless, in a measure, of what else we should miss. The result satisfied

10

us that we had made the best disposition of our time.
I wish I could give this whole letter to a description
of what we did in the way of sight-seeing the next
day after we arrived at Leamington, which is noted
in my diary as by far the most interesting day I have
spent in Europe; but how then could I speak of the
rest of this last week's experience, seeing that I have
resolved to write no more letters from this side of the
Atlantic? Brevity must be the chief characteristic
of what I say about any place hereafter.

Leamington itself is one of the prettiest places we
have seen. It is a town of comparatively modern
date, owing its sudden growth and present prosperity
to its celebrated springs, which are regarded as of
great efficiency in chronic disorders and diseases of
the skin. Hence it has become one of the most fashionable Spas in the kingdom, and its pump-room and
baths are claimed to be the most elegant in Europe.
The houses are mostly new, and many of them are
very handsome. The whole town looks more like a
picture-place than a town in the very heart of busy
smoky England, so bright and clean is everything
about it. There is hardly a house without a beautiful garden attached to it, and there are numerous
parks and pleasure grounds open to the public.
The town is built upon both banks of the little river
Leam, from which it derives its name. The streets
are bordered with great trees, and there are many attractive walks about the place. In fact one could

hardly wander in any direction without finding himself in a more beautiful country, as he would fancy, than he had ever seen before.

This much we contrived to see of Leamington the first day. Next morning we started for Warwick Castle, the stately residence of the Earl of Warwick, occupying a most picturesque situation at the southeast of the town of Warwick, on a rock washed by the Avon. The approach to the Castle is by a winding road cut through the solid rock, its walls covered with a heavy growth of ivy. The sombre stateliness of this pathway is rather oppressive for the moment, and the visitor is all the more delighted when a sudden curve reveals to his sight the grand old Castle in its most imposing aspect. Our first business, however, was with the interior. We were conducted through the magnificent rooms of the Castle, where we saw many treasures and curiosities of art which monarchs might be proud to possess. The Great Hall is considered the finest room of the kind in England. It is sixty-two feet long, forty in width, thirty-five in height, and leads to a suite of apartments which, when all open, with the Hall, form a vista of nearly three hundred and fifty feet. The Great Dining-Room, the Red Drawing-Room, the Cedar Drawing-Room, the Gilt Drawing-Room, the State Bed-Room in which Queen Elizabeth slept when on a visit to the Castle, Lady Warwick's Boudoir — these, and many other magnificent apartments, with their rich, rare, curious and costly contents, were displayed for our inspection. We took more pleasure, however, in strolling through the grounds, free from the attendance of the verjuice-faced female who described the interior to us, the grandeur of which she too fully appreciated. She was a character, by the way, was this female cicerone. She kept a sharper look-out for the fees than any other official we had yet encountered. Three or four little parties, making altogether about a dozen persons, including our party, went through the rooms together. There was one solitary gentleman, also, who might have belonged to either of the parties, as he was quite sociable, though he was a stranger to all. It was amusing to see how closely our guide watched him. She evidently suspected from the beginning that he would try and slip out without paying the customary fee. And so he did, whilst the woman was counting the heads of our party when we handed her the money. But she ran out after him and very peremptorily reminded him that he had not paid, smiling a grim significant smile when he apologetically told her that he supposed it was proper to pay at the gate.

In our wanderings about the lawns and grounds we came upon a green-house at some distance from the Castle, in which we saw the famous antique vase discovered in a lake near Adrian's villa at Tivoli, about twelve miles from Rome. It is known as the Warwick Vase, having been purchased by the late Earl

from Sir William Hamilton. It is supposed to be
more than two thousand years old, and holds about
one hundred and sixty-five gallons — a wine-cup of colossal dimensions. Quite as curious, and much more
interesting to me, were the porridge pot and meat
fork of the renowned Guy of Warwick, which are
kept in the Porter's Lodge, with his armour and other
accoutrements. The legend of this stalwart but unfortunate Crusader is too remote to excite much
enthusiasm in the present practical generation, but
we did not find it difficult to get up a good deal of
romance when the armour of the mighty King-maker,
Richard Neville, the Last of the Barons, was shown
to us. We could, apparently, go back to his times
without too great a stretch of the imagination.

What picturesque views of the stately Castle we
obtained as we strolled about the pleasure grounds!
How venerable and yet how strong it looked! We
found the dry facts of the Hand-Books as interesting
as a romance and as refreshing to the imagination,
whilst we contemplated the majestic structure. Warwick Castle is said to have been founded in 915, by
Ethelfleda, the daughter of Alfred the Great; but
it is not claimed that any of the original edifice remains, though one of the towers dates from the time
of the Conquest. It is, perhaps, the finest specimen
of the grand old houses erected by the haughty barons
of England, now in existence. Sir Walter Scott
speaks of it as the "fairest monument of ancient and

chivalrous splendor which remains uninjured by time."
Unlike most other structures of the character, it is
inhabited by its owner, and appears to be really as
comfortable a place to live in, as it is picturesque in
situation and venerable in historic associations. You
will not need, I am sure, to be reminded of the mighty
men of old, whose stronghold this Castle was, but I
am equally sure that you would be interested in the
relics of the old Barons which are preserved, carrying
one back, as it were, to the times when they lived
and moved and had their being.

From Warwick we made a pilgrimage to Stratford-
on-Avon, driving about eight miles, most of the way
in sight of the willow-margined river. I know not
whether these trees were planted by nature or by the
hand of man, but the effect is very striking. For
miles beautiful weeping willows border the stream on
either side, suggesting the thought that the Avon is
in perpetual mourning for the loss of her immortal
Bard. You will anticipate that we stopped first at
the birth-place of Shakspeare, but will not need a description of the singular-looking old house, having it,
I doubt not, familiar to your mind's eye. Over the
window is a board, like a little sign, bearing this inscription:

"THE IMMORTAL SHAKSPEARE WAS BORN IN THIS HOUSE."

Much of the exterior has been restored, but the inner rooms, especially the two chambers (in one of

which the poet was born), remain as they were originally. The walls are completely covered by the
names of visitors — crossed and recrossed like a
woman's letter — not an inch of bare space within
reach. A register is now kept wherein pilgrims can
inscribe their names. I found the signatures of many
Americans — nearly a third of all the names I should
think — in the latter pages. One gentleman, only the
day previous, had registered himself as a citizen of
Norfolk, Virginia, and added the initials C. S. A., in
the largest Roman characters. He was a Reverend,
also, but evidently did not acquiesce in the "logic
of events," and was no believer in the doctrine that
" whatever is is right."

A short distance from the house wherein Shakspeare was born, stands the church wherein he was
buried. It is a note-worthy old building, apart from
its association with the poet's memory, some portions
of it dating from the eleventh century. There are
many interesting monuments and tombs in the interior besides the celebrated bust of Shakspeare, which
is still regarded, you know, as his most trust-worthy
likeness. I carefully stepped over the stone beneath
which his ashes repose. It bears this inscription:

"GOOD FRIEND, FOR JESVS SAKE FORBEARE,
 TO DIG THE DVST ENCLOASED HEARE;
 BLESTE BE YE MAN YT. SPARES THES STONES,
 AND CVRST BE HE YT. MOVES MY BONES."

These lines are said to have been written by Shak-

speare himself. Do you believe it? They sound to
me more like the work of the stone-cutter. The most
practical and matter-of-fact of men must be moved to
eloquent thoughts, I believe, when they reverently
stand in presence of the mighty shade of Shakspeare
— for at his grave one may be said to feel his presence, so impressive are the associations which crowd
upon the spectator. If I give no utterance to my
own reflections let it be placed to my credit that I
refrained under strong temptation, because the sober
second thought told me that silence would be more
becoming in so humble an admirer of him who " was
not for a day, but for all time."

Stratford-on-Avon is one of England's oldest towns,
so old that its precise age cannot be given. As
far back as the middle of the eighth century it had
a monastery. How many years have passed since
the place had grown to its present size! Many of
the buildings are exceedingly old, and some of them
are remarkable specimens of the domestic architecture of olden times. We took dinner at the "Red
Horse," a cozy little inn which appeals to our countrymen for patronage, being "known to Americans
as Washington Irving's Hotel," according to the
landlord's card. We were served in the room which
bears the gentle writer's name, and this present writer
sat for the space of an hour in an arm chair before he
saw, by an inscription on a brass plate in the top
ledge, that it was "Washington Irving's chair."

Don't be shocked when he tells you that he did not experience any unusual sensation while seated therein.

On our return from Stratford we passed through Charlecote (pronounced *Chawcut* by the natives), a place noted for its associations with an incident in Shakspeare's life. You know the old story: how the youthful genius was caught killing a deer in Charlecote Park, and was brought before Sir Thomas Lucy, an ancestor of the present proprietor, and severely punished. I have always supposed this to be an apocryphal story, but the villagers stick to it, and still show a hill where the young scapegrace was caught by the keepers. The park is the seat of S. Lucy, Esquire. It is very extensive, finely wooded, and is plentifully stocked with deer. The mansion is spacious and handsome. It was erected in Elizabeth's time, by the prosecutor of young Shakspeare.

There was still a little daylight left when we returned to Leamington, so we concluded to visit Kenilworth before finishing the day, though that place was nearly five miles distant. It was a pleasant drive there, and we explored those interesting ruins in the dim twilight, and peopled it again in imagination with the characters still living in Scott's wonderful romance. Twilight became moonlight before we tore ourselves away from the spot. I had seen so many pictures of Kenilworth Castle, and read so many descriptions of it, that all appeared as familiar to me as though I had visited the ruins often before — a fact

10*

which would warn me not to attempt to bring the scene before my readers, even if I had the room to spare. It is not a place to be "written up" in a few hurried lines. I find unspeakable satisfaction in the thought that I have visited Kenilworth — a satisfaction which shall not be marred by the reflection that I tried to describe those romantic ruins — that lovely scenery — and failed. All readers will be glad to know that efforts are being made to preserve the ruins in their present picturesque condition. I saw a prop attached to one of the walls which would otherwise be in danger of falling. Nearly all parts of the Castle are covered with a most luxuriant growth of ivy, some of the trunks being as large around as a man could span with his arms.

It was quite late when we reached our hotel at Leamington. Just look back and remark what we had done in one day, and tell me if it was not a good hard day's work though it was only sight-seeing? I know very well that we ought to have spent a week instead of a day in exploring these places — but what is one to do when his time is as limited as mine?

We had not much help from our Jehu that day. He was not very communicative — rather a misanthropic old chap, in fact. Usually we had found that our drivers were quite knowing characters — but this one was an exception to the rule. I tried hard to draw him out, but it was as difficult to get any information from him as to unearth a badger. He never said "Yes" or "No" to anything, nor yet that he didn't know. "I dessay, Sir," was his usual reply. Once only did he volunteer a remark, and that was at the beginning of our drive. Pointing to the river, he said "that's the Haven, Sir." "What haven?" I asked, quite innocently. "The river Haven, Sir," he replied. And then it occurred to me that "Haven" was Warwickshire for Avon. Perhaps the old fellow thought I was quizzing him in not understanding his meaning at the first moment, and for this reason was so reticent the rest of the day; but he was deluded if he did, for there was no touch of mockery in my thoughts.

There are many other interesting places in the vicinity of Leamington to which we should have paid visits if time had permitted. You will notice that I have told you nothing about Guy's Cliffe or Stoneleigh Abbey, places which every tourist who stops at Leamington expects to visit. Sad to say, my haste was too urgent to admit of any further rambles in that delightful locality, and therefore you must try and be content with what I have told you.

After leaving Leamington the first place at which we stopped was Chester, which claims to be the oldest city in England, some (Chester people, of course) going so far as to say that it was a city before the Roman conquest. The place has certainly a very old look. Many of the houses are singularly constructed, having porticoes running along the front the whole

length of a street, affording a covered walk to pedes-
trians. Shops and warehouses are beneath, on a level
with the street.   I noticed a somewhat similar feature
in the buildings at Berne, in Switzerland. Chester
Castle is supposed to have been erected in the time
of William the Conqueror. Only a portion of the
original building remains, and that has been lately repaired. The Cathedral is the oldest-looking church I
have seen in Europe, and one of the most interesting.
It is blackened with age. We were shown some por-
tions which were supposed to be of the fifth century
— but not warranted; other parts, quite authentic, of
the eleventh century. We were conducted through
it by an amusing old gentlemen, one of the most
original characters we have encountered. His description of the Cathedral was interspersed with the
quaintest observations, more remarkable for oddity
than piety. "The old lady is very bad to-day, Sir,"
he whispered to me. I turned to the two ladies in
the party, thinking at first he alluded to one of them;
but it was plain that neither could fairly be called
old or bad-looking. "What old lady?" I demanded.
"The poor old lady up there," replied he, pointing to
a grotesque figure of an old woman carved on one of
the beams, with hands clasped before her, face dis-
torted, and form doubled up, as though she was suffering from a dreadful stomach-ache.

The Cathedral is built of the red sandstone found
in the vicinity — a soft stone which appears to wash

away, but holds the mortar well. The sharp edges of all the stones have been rounded off by the elements, giving the building a very singular appearance. Another church (St. John's) is built of similar material, but looks even more venerable than the Cathedral. It was founded, according to local history, by Ethelred, in the seventh century. The most ancient portion of this church is a mass of ivy-grown ruins. Some idea of how long they have been ruins may be gathered from a.very curious circumstance which is sure to attract the attention of visitors. A large elm tree stands directly under one of the arches, branching off at the top and reaching a great height above the wall, looking as if the arch was built over the fork of the tree. How long the arch had stood before the tree began to grow, cannot be known, though I dare say it would not be difficult to determine the present age of the tree. The interior of St. John's has lately been restored, and proves to be of a later date than the ruins. It is considered one of the finest specimens of the early Norman style of architecture extant. There are many old buildings in Chester, as curious and interesting to the antiquarian, perhaps, as the two churches I have mentioned; but these are the most noted objects with ordinary travelers, and should not be overlooked.

We did not leave Chester until we had visited the Park and grounds of Eaton Hall, a superb mansion, built in florid Gothic style, and belonging to the Mar-

quis of Westminster. It is beautifully situated on the
banks of the Dee, between three and four miles from
Chester, and is said to be a favorite residence with its
owner. Well it may be, for a more delightful place
could hardly be imagined. The hall is furnished with
great splendor. The private chapel is considered one
of the prettiest in England. Driving through the
Park gave us something of an idea of the magnitude
of the estate. It extends more than eight miles in one
direction; a nice little homestead certainly, with which
a man might be almost content, one would fancy, if
that beatific state is ever to be attained in this vain
world. But this is only a tithe of the landed property
belonging to the Marquis; and he has many mansions
besides Eaton Hall, with the largest income, too, it
is said, of any gentleman in England. Poor man,
what a burden it all must be to him! Who would
not be willing to relieve him of a part of it?

Our next stopping place was Liverpool, but the
weather was so abominable on the way there and
during our stay, that we were not inclined to see
much of that place. We could not help noting, however, that it is an extremely busy city, more like New
York than any other place we have seen. The great
docks of Liverpool are the chief boast of her citizens.
We plodded our way about them in the driving rain,
and found them well worth a visit. We saw one
great vessel, an East-Indiaman, being unladen of rice,
and could not help admiring (in the reverse sense of

the term) the slow old-fashioned method in which the grain was handled. I wish some of our great Elevators were at work in Liverpool, just to show her people how we do business out in the western world; but if you keep burning them down, I fear we shall have none to spare.* I must say a good word for the Adelphi Hotel, because we found it one of the best, the most comfortable and home-like, of all the hotels we have tried in Europe. So many Americans stop at Liverpool, on their arrival in and departure from England, that this fact would be worth printing even if a suspicion of puffery should attach to the mention of it — a suspicion that would be entirely groundless, I need not assure you.

From Liverpool we went per rail to Holyhead, getting a peep at some of the most beautiful scenery of the northern coast of Wales, through which we passed on the way, and riding across the great Tubular Bridge over the mouth of the river Conway, and the still greater one across the Menai Strait. The latter bridge is considered one of the most stupendous achievements of engineering science, and I regarded it as a piece of good fortune to travel through it and get a fair view of the situation. At Holyhead we took a fine steamer for Kingstown, doing the sixty-four miles across the Irish Channel in less than four

---

* In the space of less than four years previous to the date of this letter, eleven great Elevators were burned down in Buffalo, involving a loss of nearly two millions of dollars.

hours, notwithstanding that the sea was rough, and there was a head wind. I had never before realized how wide a gulf there is between the Emerald Isle and England, though I knew that Irishmen wished it was wider still. You will think it strange, perhaps, that I mused much over the thought of Ireland being twice as far from England as England is from France, while I was watching for the first glimpse of the shore. I ought to have been tolerably familiar with this geographical fact before, and I dare say, when it comes to the point, I did know that much, only from habit had forgotten it. It may be that I was conscious, in that uncomfortable interval, of certain rather uncharitable views I had long entertained with regard to a class of Irish agitators in America. At any rate those sixty-four miles of rough sea voyaging inspired me with more sympathy for the object at which the Fenians aim than I had ever felt before. Set that down as a candid admission, and give me credit for it. But not too much credit though, for it may have been nothing but a stomach repentance, after all. I believe it is Mr. Beecher who speaks of people often fancying they have got religion when they are only bilious. Perhaps it was something similar that ailed me when I was enjoying the new-born feeling of sympathy with the hopeless scheme of the Fenians. Certainly if there be any bile in a man it is likely to get agitated in crossing the Channel.

We did not tarry at Kingstown, though there is

much about the place to invite the traveler to halt awhile, to say nothing about the disinclination he must feel to continue his journey after a stormy passage across the Channel. The town is a very pretty one, and there is nice sea-bathing there, facts which have made it quite a fashionable summer resort of late years. We, however, proceeded straight to Dublin, less than an hour's ride. And here we are, in the capital of Ireland, expecting to spend the last week before sailing in convenient little excursions about the green isle. Two days in Dublin, one or two in County Wicklow — a region that embraces much of Ireland's most beautiful scenery, — the other three or four at the Lakes of Killarney and in Cork (from whence we sail next Thursday) will probably make up a week of the busiest and most enjoyable traveling and sight-seeing in our experience. If I tell you anything of all this, though, it must be in a letter written after I reach home. Meantime, I hopefully and thankfully say " Good-bye."

XIII.

DUBLIN AND SOME OF ITS SIGHTS. — AN EXCURSION TO COUN-
TY WICKLOW IN A JAUNTING-CAR, WITH A "TOO HANDY"
DRIVER, AND WHAT CAME OF IT. — THE LAKES OF KIL-
LARNEY. — THE GAP OF DUNLOE. — KATE KEARNEY AND
HER DESCENDANTS. — SCENERY ABOUT THE LAKES. — IN-
NISFALLEN ISLAND. — CORK. — BLARNEY CASTLE AND THE
BLARNEY STONE. — START FOR THE SHIP. — OMINOUS
WORDS.

BUFFALO, October 11th, 1866.

To write a letter to you, dear *Commercial,* now
that I am at home, makes me feel like old Solomon in
the play, who had correspondence from all parts of
the world — written by himself; but, having made a
sort of half promise in my last to complete the record of my experience in Europe, and finding that
some of my readers are disposed to remind me of that
circumstance, kindly expressing an interest in the
matter, I will try and keep my word, and even go a
little further, and bring my account down to our arrival in New York, at the risk of doing a work of
supererogation.

I find that I told you nothing of Dublin, except that our party had arrived there. We spent only two days in the Irish capital, and I cannot, therefore, pretend to tell you much about it, except as to general impressions. It is a handsome city, with many stately buildings and fine wide streets, but a very dull place, I should think, so far as business goes. It was almost painful for active-minded Americans to see how deserted the streets looked. One street in particular, and that one of the finest (Sackville street), shows much less traffic than is seen on our Main street, though it is about three times as broad, and Dublin has nearly thrice as many inhabitants as Buffalo. I know not why it was, but our whole party certainly were victims to the blues all the while we were there, a circumstance which may have given a sombre coloring to our impressions of Dublin; or else the knowledge that the ancient city is actually in a rapid decline — its population steadily decreasing * and its business " going to the dogs "— made us view the place with the sort of melancholy interest with which one always contemplates the hectic fading beauty of a consumptive woman. We found this impression could not be eradicated, even when we took

---

* What is true of Dublin, in this respect, appears to be true of the whole island. The Registrar-General's half-yearly Report on Births, Deaths and Marriages in Ireland, shows that in the quarter ending the 30th of June last the number of births was 38,816; of deaths 24,763, and of emigrants 41,124; the result of which is a diminution of the population of Ireland by 27,071 in the three months.

our first ride on a jaunting-car, though the novelty of
the situation and the constant care required to hold
our seats, would have kept us merry as well as busy
in any other place. You know what a jaunting-car
is, I suppose — a sort of little omnibus turned inside
out and minus the roof — an abominable invention,
exactly the reverse of what it ought to be. A narrow
seat is suspended over each wheel and there is a nar-
rower board to rest the feet upon. You feel certain
you will pitch off unless you hang on for dear life, or
are hardened to the performance. We sat, two on
one side, back to back with two on the other side, in
a very unsocial fashion. A fifth (but only a little
one) was perched on the space between, with his
back to the driver, who has the only tolerably comfortable seat. Perhaps I am rather more prejudiced
against them now than I was at my first experience,
for it was only a day or two later that a nearly serious accident happened to some of our party, including myself, arising out of the carelessness of a wild
Irish driver of one of these vehicles. But more of
this by-and-bye, in its proper place.

Our first drive in Dublin was to the Phœnix Park,
a splendid and almost too large inclosure, containing
nearly eighteen hundred acres, and affording many
fine but rather lonesome drives, so few people are to
be met on the way. The Park is finely wooded, and
plentifully stocked with deer as tame as sheep ; but
it struck me that less extensive grounds would be

more enjoyable as a public park for so small a city as Dublin. The most conspicuous object in the Park is the Wellington Testimonial, an immense quadrangular truncated obelisk, erected by his fellow-townsmen of Dublin in 1817, to commemorate the victories of the Great Duke, at a cost of over one hundred thousand dollars. The work was done entirely by Irish artisans, and a very handsome piece of work it is. On our way to this spot we had passed an enclosure within which were rows of cannon pointed toward the city, which they commanded; an unpleasant reminder that the authorities did not feel " quite at home " in the Irish capital. The palace occupied by the Viceroy is not far from the entrance to the Park. It is not an imposing building, by any means — indeed, I think it would be regarded as rather shabby were it in the neighborhood of Madison Square, New York.

Soon tiring of the Park, we turned back and drove about the city, taking hasty glances at many fine public buildings, of which Dublin has more in proportion to its size than any other city we have visited. We had no time to examine the interiors, and you will therefore be spared any further particulars, except in respect to St. Patrick's Cathedral, which we did enter, and pretty thoroughly explore, having curiosity to see the church upon the restoration of which one wealthy man (Mr. Guinness, the great brewer,) had spent more than half a million of dollars. One cannot, of course, very well judge of the magnitude of the re-

pairs unless he has seen the Cathedral in its former
state; but all can now attest that it is a most noble
and beautiful church, in perfect condition, yet retain-
ing much of the venerable appearance bestowed upon
it by the passing ages.

It is as well attested as any fact can be which has
come down to us from those remote times, that St.
Patrick erected a place of worship, which existed for
some centuries, on the site of the present Cathedral;
for it is on record that Gregory of Scotland and his
followers attended worship in it, in the year 890, more
than four hundred years after St. Patrick's time. A
well was near the spot, in which the patron saint bap-
tized his converts. The present Cathedral was begun
in the twelfth century by Archbishop Comyn, and we
were shown parts of it which remain to this day un-
altered and almost untouched by time. A small portion is pointed out as the remains of the original
church erected by St. Patrick, but the fact is not insisted upon. The interior is very beautiful, and it is
decorated with many exceedingly interesting monuments. The unpretending slabs which denote the
places where Dean Swift and his "Stella" rest, "after
life's fitful fever," peacefully, side by side, will surely
attract the attention of the visitor.

What a singular compound was Swift! One hardly
knows whether to admire or despise him, most. The
janitor who conducted us told some stories about him
which I had never heard before, though I dare say

they are familiar enough to most readers. Did you ever hear how he got his appointment as Dean of St. Patrick's? There was a certain lady, a great admirer of Swift's, who possessed much family influence at Court. "Get me made Dean," said Swift to this lady, "and I'll marry you whenever you are ready." The lady exerted herself, and Swift was appointed. He did not appear to be in any hurry to keep his word, and she therefore waited upon him and demanded a fulfillment of the bargain. "Certainly," said the Dean, "What day is it to take place?" An early day was named and the Dean promised to be at the Church. The lady was prompt, and the Dean was present. "Where is the bridegroom?" asked he of the lady. "Yourself, surely," she replied. "Did you not promise to marry me?" "Yes," responded the Dean, "and so I will, now or any time, for nothing— *but I didn't promise to find the husband!*" Our conductor laughed as long and loud when he finished the story as though he never had told about the heartless cheat before.

Near the resting place of Swift is a very singular monument, attracting attention by its cumbersome oddity. It is a large group erected to Boyle, Earl of Cork, in 1639, of black marble and wood-carving, gilded and painted, representing the Earl and his wife in reclining positions surrounded by their sixteen children. What a pleasant little family! There was much more to interest us in St. Patrick's, but a great deal has escaped my memory. It belongs to the Reformed religion now, but, as our driver told us when we came out, "the Fanian boys say the Catholics shall have it again." He was a character, by the way, that driver of ours. Intelligent and witty, with a splendid, rich, but not vulgar brogue, very much like Collins, the Irish Comedian. He was inclined to be non-committal as to his politics, but we soon discovered that his sympathies were with the "Fanian boys." Such, indeed, so far as we could observe, was the case with nearly every man of his class we encountered in Ireland.

We went to another Cathedral, "Christ's Church," the vaults of which, according to the "Black Book of Christ's Church," were constructed by the Danes long before St. Patrick visited the Island. It is claimed that he afterward celebrated mass in one of them. The present church, however, is described as "of comparatively modern date," being only eight or nine hundred years old! I wonder what age a church must have to be styled ancient, according to this. From Christ's Church to the Cemetery was not a long drive, but the latter proved to be so beautiful a place that we should have felt repaid had the distance been much greater. Our driver had only asked if we would like to see O'Connell's tomb, and we were not prepared, therefore, to find much else that was interesting. The grounds, which are quite extensive, are so tastefully laid out and so well preserved,

there are so many flowers and hedges and trees, and
the walks are so prettily bordered, that the spot
makes as cheerful a burial place as one could desire.
We found that nearly all the visitors registered their
impressions of the place, and they were unanimous
upon this point. Few of the graves but had some
token of love, in the shape of baskets of flowers or
wreaths, left there by friends or relatives of the de-
ceased. O'Connell's monument is a very conspicuous
object, but not a beautiful one, nor hardly an appropriate one it seems to me, though there may be some
significance, beyond my appreciation, in its resem-
blance to the peculiar ancient round towers which are
so numerous in most parts of Ireland. It is built of
granite, is upwards of one hundred and sixty feet in
height, and surmounted by a cross eight feet high
weighing about two tons. There is a vault beneath
the tower, intended as a receptacle for the great
Agitator's ashes, which at present repose in another
part of the grounds surrounded by a deep ditch. A
more interesting tomb to me was that of the great
orator, Curran. It is built of Irish granite, and is a
fac-simile of the celebrated monument of Scipio Bar-
batiens.

From Dublin we made an excursion to County
Wicklow, proceeding by rail to Bray (about twelve
miles), a very pretty watering place which has lately
grown into great repute, and where tourists with
plenty of time make their headquarters for several

11

days, for the reason that many pleasant excursions
can be made from it.   We could give only one day to`
it, however, and had therefore taken an early start.
Arrived at Bray, we were soon provided with a car,
though not without a great deal of bother from rival
drivers, who bantered us and blackguarded one another with amusing volubility.   One fellow followed
us even after we had selected our car. " Faith, it's
sorry for ye I am," he said, as we were about to start.
" Ye'll never get back alive," he added ;. " that black-
guard is always killin' somebody with his carelessness,
he is."   I was surprised that our driver did not return
abuse for abuse; but concluded that what he lacked
in ready wit he made up in steadiness, which was by
far the most desirable quality.   The route we proposed was said to be thirty miles in length. " Can
your horse do it by five o'clock ? " I asked the driver.
"Too handy, y'r han'r," was the reply, and off we
started.

We were bound first for "The Dargle," a glen about
a mile in length, through which the river Dargle flows.
We explored this glen on foot, obtaining many charming views on the way.   The ravine is beautifully
wooded, the rocky banks of the river rising in some
places as high as three hundred feet, thickly covered
with native wild wood and graceful ferns.   Seen from
above, the glen is a lovely combination of rugged
rock and many-tinted foliage, the sparkling stream
plashing and dashing its way along at the bottom.

There is one bold projecting point, called the "Lover's Leap," from which the best view is obtained. Of course there is a story connected with this spot, which gives it the name — but not a very probable one, equally of course. From the Dargle we drove to Enniskerry, a remarkably pretty village, the property of Lord Powerscourt, situated in a deep valley, watered by a small stream, and a favorite place of resort with Dublin people. Thence about three miles, at a rattling pace, to Powerscourt, driving through the beautiful demesne, nearly eight hundred acres of which are enclosed. The whole estate contains twenty-six thousand acres. The family is said to be one of the most popular in Ireland. Much account is made of the Waterfall, whither we wended, but I think Americans are apt to be disappointed in Waterfalls, as we have the largest and most imposing, both natural and artificial, in the world. Niagara is not more supreme in this respect than are the other kind we have so many of to show. We saw the Powerscourt Waterfall in its most favorable aspect, a great deal of rain having recently fallen, (as we knew to our sorrow)— but yet, though pretty, there was not much of it. In dry weather it must be a trifling affair. George the Fourth once made a visit to Powerscourt, and in order to make sure of a good supply of water a large tank was built at the top of the hill, but his fat majesty did not take the trouble to go to the spot after all.

Just as we had seen all we desired in the neighbor-

hood of the Waterfall it began to rain, and it was
time, therefore, to think of returning to Bray. We
took another route back, passing through the Rocky
Valley, a very strange passage of about a mile in
length, enclosed by high mountains, with huge wierd-
looking rocks scattered in every direction. Shortly
after, we stopped at a little road-side inn, the name of
which I forget, but it is quite celebrated in the neighborhood, humble as it looked. Unpromising as was
its exterior, we found a tolerably clean little back
room, and were soon served with a capital lunch of the
best brown bread we ever tasted — a luxury for which
the landlady is famous — with sweet, golden-hued but-
ter, Cheshire cheese and water-cresses. Bottled ale of
the best was not wanting, and something stronger
and hotter was prescribed, and taken too, "to keep
out the cold rain." When we left, hearty cheers and
best wishes were given to "the Americans," and our
driver was exhorted to do his best for us.

Was there any significance in that hint, I wonder?
At any rate it seemed to spur our "too handy" Jehu
to unwonted exertions. He was evidently bent upon
showing "the Americans" a taste of what an Irish
horse could do, and drove us along at a break-neck
pace, regardless of consequences. Having to hold up
umbrellas it was all we could do to hang on the seat
by the skin of our — teeth, I was about to say, but
that seems to be a rather far-fetched simile — when
we were going over level ground; but when the fel-

low drove full tilt down a steep hill, and turned a sharp corner at the bottom without slacking speed, you will not be surprised to hear that we who were on the side which caught the full momentum of the swing, were flung violently from the car, alighting, providentially, in the softest and dirtiest mud to be found in Ireland. The situation was too serious to be ludicrous. When I scrambled up there were two others to look after, who, I feared, had sustained severe injuries. Fortunately no bones were broken, though all were in a sorry plight. It was a mystery how so much mud could be gathered on one person. A cottage hard by afforded us the opportunity to wash and scrape and clean up a little. The driver was so frightened, and so penitent, and we were so thankful at our escape without broken bones, that we did not punish the fellow as I still strongly suspect he deserved. I found it hard to exercise that spirit of forgiveness to which I was exhorted by the friend who, having sat on the other side of the car, didn't get upset. He was sure the reckless fellow was actuated by the best of motives — merely wanted to surprise us — which he certainly succeeded in doing. I questioned very much, though, whether my friend would have been so charitable in his construction of the driver's conduct if he had sat on my side of the car. However, as I said, we let it go, and drove back to Bray as quickly as possible, consistent with safety. We paid for the nice little dinner we had ordered at the hotel but did not wait to eat it, preferring to take the first train back to Dublin, quite satisfied that we had had enough of Ireland for one day. I don't remember seeing either of the party on a jaunting car after that incident.

The following day we took the rail for Killarney, a long and tedious journey only enlivened here and there with glimpses of beautiful scenery. The town has one long street, with a lot of dirty offshoots, and is about as dingy and ugly a place as can be imagined. The lakes are a mile or two from the town, and the hotels are located upon their banks — good hotels, too, where the traveler soon finds himself at home. We stopped at the "Victoria," and did not regret it, though I believe the "Lake House" and one or two others are considered equally good. The two houses I have named are situated on the banks of the principal lake, about a mile apart, and both command beautiful views. I suppose the lake region looks all the more charming after passing through the squalid town; at any rate our first impression was that in all our wanderings we had stumbled upon no more delightful spot.

The next day after our arrival was a blessed day of rest, and we did rest and were thankful, too, I hope. But we were up bright and early on Monday morning, for we had a long trip planned which would take the whole day to accomplish. Our design was to drive to the head of the lakes and return by boat, an excursion which would enable us to see more of the country

in one day than would be possible in any other way.
All arrangements for this trip and many others, can
be made with the proprietors of the hotels, who have
fixed tariffs for all the charges — a plan that relieves
the tourist of a great deal of trouble. We took a carriage (no more jaunting-cars, mind you!) to the Gap of
Dunloe, driving several miles before that pass was
reached. We had barely started before we were beset
with women on the road offering bog-oak trinkets for
sale. One, more persevering than the rest, ran quite
half a mile beside the carriage, though we were going
at a good round pace; and she talked faster than she
ran. Seeing that she would not be denied, I stopped
the carriage and purchased some trifle, and was much
laughed at for my pains when it was discovered later
in the day that I had paid about double price for the
ornament. However, it was worth the money to see
the woman spit on the coin "for luck," and to hear
her voluble outpouring of thanks. It was her first
sale that morning, and now she would be sure of "the
bright good luck" all the week. We soon had occasion to think it unfortunate that we started so early,
for, being the first party that had passed, we were
beset with double importunity from the whole ragged
tribe to give them a good start in the week's business.
One hardly knows whether to be annoyed or amused
at the pertinacity of these highway merchants — but
after all the loose change is gone I think the former
sentiment gains the ascendancy.

Just at the entrance to the Gap stands the cottage where the famous beauty, Kate Kearney, lived. It is now occupied by a grand-daughter of hers, still claiming the same name and having a remarkably large family, all active despoilers of travelers' purses. I think it was a great-grand-daughter who paid particular attentions to me. She was a big, strapping girl, with not much of her ancestor's beauty unless it was in her bold, handsome, dark eyes. It was quite unnecessary for me to "beware of her eye," though I did pay for a drink of goat's milk and "mountain dew" — the "rale stuff" she said — which I didn't drink. Such a crowd of urgent half-beggars gathered about us at this point, all insisting upon our buying something — lace, bog-wood ornaments, or other trumpery — that we were glad to break away and mount horses for the passage through the Gap, as the carriage could proceed no further. All did mount horses, I say, but one dismounted again, very quickly, for he soon discovered that he could not ride a horse with ease or safety. It was quite a little cavalcade that rode gaily through the Gap of Dunloe that morning, but the solitary pedestrian still thinks he had the best of it, for his were much the best opportunities to note the singular scenery of that four miles of narrow mountain defile.

A little stream courses through the glen, widening at different points into five little lakes, each with a characteristic name, and a legend, too, of course.

One, the "Black Lough," is the spot where St. Patrick is said to have banished the last Irish snake. The traveler gazes with a touch of awe at the lofty projecting rocks which enclose the narrow path on either side, threatening to tumble over at every step, bringing destruction with their fall. When we emerged from the Gap, we were within sight of the Black Valley, which we did not explore for want of time, though we could see something of its gloomy yet picturesque aspect. An imaginative writer thus speaks of this valley: "Had there been at the bottom among the rugged masses of black rock, some smoke and flame instead of water, we might have imagined we were looking into the entrance to the infernal regions." Oh, the sturdy beggars that beset the rough and rugged path I traveled that day! What mingled perseverance and impudence they displayed in their charges upon my sympathies! I almost wished I was on horseback again. One stout woman, "a poor widow with six small children," trudged along by my side nearly half a mile, trying to wheedle a sixpence out of me; and when I told her that I had no silver left she offered to change a sovereign for me! I borrowed a sixpence to give her, thinking the coolness of the thing worth the money, though, as I told her, I was almost ashamed to offer so insignificant a sum to so considerable a capitalist.

Soon after we passed the Gap we found the boat which had been sent through the lakes to take us home

11*

that way. It was manned by four stout oarsmen, and a bugler who was cockswain as well. The landlord had sent us an appetizing lunch, to which we were by this time able to do ample justice. We were then in the Upper Lake, a beautiful sheet of water, not quite three miles in length by less than a mile in breadth, but containing twelve little islands, each a gem. The prettiest is called Arbutus Island, from being almost entirely covered with that beautiful plant. Majestic mountains enclose the placid Lake, and, as we glided along, the scene was one continued enjoyment. Near the Long Range — a little river of about two miles in length, and through which we rowed to the Middle Lake — a mountain called the Eagle's Nest rears its lofty head seven hundred feet almost perpendicularly above the water. Our cockswain landed on the opposite shore, and, standing behind a rock, played some tunes on his bugle. The original notes were quite lost to us, but the echoes from the Eagle's Nest were very distinct and musical.

I cannot tell all I remember of that delightful excursion, for want of room. I know that we thought the Meeting of the Waters, just as we reached the Middle Lake, a more remarkable view than anything we had seen yet; that the Middle Lake was prettier than the Upper; and when we reached the Lower Lake, we thought that more beautiful still. The last is quite an imposing sheet of water, five miles long by three broad. More than thirty islands dot its surface.

On Ross Island the ruins of the Castle once inhabited by the O'Donaghue of the Lakes, call to mind a legend about that Chieftain which our bugler relates in a pleasant brogue. The most charming spot on the Lake to my mind is that part called Glenna Bay. Here we landed, and looked over a picturesque little cottage belonging to Lady Kenmare. It was not forgotten to inform us that Queen Victoria took lunch in this cottage when she visited the lakes. The view from this spot was so enchanting that we lingered on it almost too long, and had not, therefore, as much time left as we wished when we stopped at Innisfallen Island, the most interesting of them all, where we saw the ruins of an old Abbey said to be founded in the year 600 by St. Finian, who must be the patron saint that has so many followers now-a-days. What pretty glades and lawns, what grand old trees and shrubs — (here is the largest holly tree in the world) — what magnificent views we saw whilst on that island I cannot pretend to describe. Did not Moore write of "Sweet Innisfallen"? Then why should I? Yet it will be a satisfaction to me to "drop into poetry" like Mr. Wegg, as I take my leave of that enchanting spot:

> "Sweet Innisfallen, long shall dwell
> In memory's dream that sunny smile,
> Which o'er thee on that evening fell
> When first I saw thy fairy isle."

Half an hour's steady rowing landed us at the hotel.

What a long day of pleasure it had been! Nearly five hours of it had been spent on the waters — the boatmen singing — and dancing too, at such times as we landed, the wildest, maddest Irish jigs — the bugler playing — passing boats hailing us, giving cheers for the Americans — and all going "merry as a marriage bell." Nor were the songs of old Ireland the only songs heard upon Killarney's lakes that day. John Brown went marching on, Tramp, tramp, and Johnny came marching home, while the Star Spangled Banner in triumph did wave — at least we sung that it did!

If the next day had been fine, we should have made other excursions from Killarney, but two pleasant days in succession are rarely seen in Ireland, I am told. Rain, however, is no great detriment to railway traveling, so we went down to Cork, and had one day longer there than we expected. This we improved by driving about the city and to Blarney Castle, about five miles out. We thought Cork a handsome city, and with a more active business aspect than Dublin, but had no time to make notes about it. Blarney claimed more attention. There is but little left of the Castle, except one massive tower, about one hundred and twenty feet in height. It is almost completely covered with ivy, and is a picturesque ruin enough, but nothing remarkable. It's the Blarney Stone that gives it such notoriety, and brings most of the visitors, no doubt. A long flat stone, held in its place on a projecting buttress at the summit of the tower by two iron bands clasped around it — that's the Blarney Stone. To kiss it, it is necessary to project the body over the wall, holding on by the iron bands, a feat of some danger. "Father Prout" sang of the Stone in this wise:

> "There is a stone there,
> That whoever kisses,
> Oh, he never misses
>   To grow eloquent.
> 'Tis he may clamber
> To a lady's chamber,
> Or become a member
>   Of Parliament.

> "A clever spouter
> He'll sure turn out, or
> An out and outer
>   To be let alone!
> Don't hope to hinder him
> Or to bewilder him,
> Sure he's a pilgrim
>   From the Blarney Stone."

Having read this you will perhaps wonder I didn't attempt to accomplish the feat. A word in your ear — don't mention it — I had been often told that I must have kissed the Blarney Stone, before I ever saw it — and thought, therefore, it was not necessary to risk my neck!

The pleasure grounds near the Castle are the celebrated Groves of Blarney, which are so charming. It needs the song, though, to make one think them anything extraordinary.   A fat old woman keeps the keys of the Castle.   She has done so for more than thirty years, she says.   A fat old fellow shows the Groves.   Both expect fees, and a friend, whose lingering behind I had not been able to account for, told me the old woman said that gentlemen who did not kiss the Stone usually kissed her instead, a fee I am sure he paid though he denies it to this day.

Back to Cork, and next morning down to Queenstown — noting nothing.   Too full of preparations for the voyage home.   It was stormy weather, and somewhat doubtful whether the steamer could get in.   The voyage commenced inauspiciously.   As I was leaving the office for the little steamer which was waiting to take us to the ship, the agent called the attention of a gentleman to the barometer, and said these ominous words — the last I heard on shore: "My God, look how the glass is running down!   There is bad weather ahead!"

XIV.

DESCRIPTIVE OF THE VOYAGE HOME, AND NARRATING SOME
INCIDENTS AND DISASTERS WHICH HAPPENED DURING A
GREAT STORM.

BUFFALO, October 19th, 1866.

It was not a very encouraging omen with which to
commence a voyage across the Atlantic — that remark
of the man who looked at the barometer, as quoted at
the end of my last letter, — and I confess that, though
generally disposed to look on the bright side of things,
those ominous words fell on my ear with a rather
chilling effect.   In truth, the weather was already bad
enough.   We had for several hours been watching the
harbor from the window of the hotel, looking for the
arrival of the steamer, and noting with something of
apprehension the unfavorable aspect of the weather
which became more and more unfavorable every minute.   When she did arrive, at length, it was raining
hard, and blowing harder.   I had got completely wet
through as well as bothered and perplexed, in looking
after baggage, and had lost my dinner besides.   I

doubt if Mark Tapley himself would not have found it difficult to keep up an appearance of jollity under such discouraging circumstances. I made an effort, however, and believe it succeeded tolerably well. To board the ship was a work of some difficulty. The little steamer which carried us to her side was bobbing about in a very aggravating way, and it was partly a lift, partly a shove, partly a slip and partly a jump that landed us on the deck of that A 1 steamer, on the twentieth day of September — of all the days in the year the most inauspicious for Atlantic voyages, as I have since been told.

Nor was there much to encourage us in the first appearance of matters on board the ship. She was over-crowded with passengers. Trunks and boxes blocked the way in the passages between the cabins, and when we found our rooms they were occupied by other people. It was not pleasant. The ship was on her course before we had obtained possession of our rooms, and it was not an easy matter to get settled then, for she soon began to rock in a manner very trying to the stomach. It is a great comfort to have all one's little conveniences nicely arranged in one's cabin, and I advise travelers, therefore, to get their rooms fairly in order before the ship starts, for there is no telling how soon they may want to lie down, quite careless of appearances.

Before night at least two-thirds of the passengers were sea-sick. What dreadful sickness there was in my own party, and how busy and anxious a time it was for me, who, fortunately, had not even a qualm, and was therefore able to be of some use — this is not the place to tell. My business is to try and tell something about that memorable voyage home — a voyage that will not be forgotten, I am sure, by any one of the passengers. The wind was against us from the start. The ship fought her way along bravely, in spite of it, making pretty fair progress the first three days, though the weather was rougher, and the sea ran higher, all the time, than I had seen it on the voyage out. Thus far, however, it was simply rough, disagreeable weather; unpleasant, but not dangerous. The great storm commenced on the evening of Sunday, the twenty-third of September, and it proved to be one of the longest and most violent that ever swept over the Atlantic.

The night of Sunday was a terrible one. The ship was kept on her course in the teeth of the gale. She rocked and pitched so fearfully that sleep was impossible. But the rocking and pitching did not cause the worst sensation. Every few minutes the ship would give a great plunge, and then the screw came out of the water and made a tremendous noise — a horrible, craunching noise, which thrilled through the nerves of the passengers like an actual spasm of pain. The ship would writhe and quiver, and groan almost, at these times, as though she were a great living creature having one of her largest teeth wrenched out, and one half expected to hear her scream in agony. Morning found the passengers a wretched set of beings, most of them sick and frightened. The scene in the cabins was one of dire confusion. It was next to impossible to keep on one's feet, or on a seat, indeed, without a tight grasp upon something. Every effort was made to preserve the regular routine of the meals, but the few who were bold enough, or unconcerned enough, to try to eat, made poor work of it. The gale increased in fury all day. The captain, a daring and pugnacious sort of man, with a great reputation for making quick voyages, appeared to be determined to fight the elements. He kept the ship on her course, though the fearful gale was dead against her, and drove the poor vessel along, in spite of the blinding blows of the waves which smote her in the face and battered her, right and left, every minute. As she tore along through the dreadful roaring waters, I thought her like a wild horse, and the waves like a pack of hungry wolves with frothing jaws leaping at her throat.

At about ten o'clock of Monday night the gale seemed to have reached its height. It was then that a tremendous sea broke over the stern of the ship, crushed the pilot-house like an egg-shell, and shattered the steering-wheels into a thousand splinters. The men at the wheel were dashed out of the house and swept along the decks like toys. This moment was the crisis of our fate. It was a fortunate circumstance — to us it seemed a Providence — that the ship was provided with an extra pilot-house and steering apparatus near the middle of the deck, being the only ship of the line, I believe, which is thus equipped. The brave man who had charge of the wheel rushed into the broken house again, through the surging waters, and put a brake on the rudder; then ran forward and reported the disaster to the captain, who immediately manned the extra wheel. The safety of the ship and her passengers and crew, was due, under God, to the presence of mind exhibited by this brave seaman. Had he been less prompt or less plucky we should have been lost. And so we should if another great wave had struck the ship in the interval when she was without the use of a rudder. We were, indeed, within a minute of destruction.

Up to this time our captain had been fighting the storm. He was the kind of man to return blow for blow, and never give in. He had kept the ship up to the work, facing the wind, and making her take the punishment as he would himself, like a man. But the contest was manifestly too unequal, and at length more prudent counsels prevailed, and the ship was "hove to." The storm did not abate, however, for nearly twenty-four hours longer. The passengers, even the boldest of them, began to lose heart at the prolonged struggle. No outcry, no complaints, no weeping, were heard, but every face wore a grave and an anxious expression. The whole of Tuesday was

passed in this way. None of the passengers were
able to get out upon deck to see what was the state
of the ship. One of the cabin doors was bolted, and
men stood guard at the other, watching opportunities
to let the servants out and in, as was necessary,
fastening the door when a lurch of the ship brought a
huge wave over that side. At such moments we
could catch a glimpse of the angry sea, alive with
"cruel, crawling foam," hissing and seething, rushing
at the ship in great mountainous waves, as if eager to
swallow us all at one vast gulp — huge waves that
shut out all view of the sky. The roar of the tempest
drowned all other sounds, even though we heard it
only through closed doors. Shouts became as whispers. Men tried to talk, and most of them wished to
say something cheering to each other: but it was almost as difficult to speak as it was to hear — and more
difficult than either was it to appear cheerful. The
constant recurrence of that dreadful noise when the
screw came out of the water — a noise that was neither
a grating, a clanking, a pounding, or a ringing noise,
but a harrowing commingling of them all — kept all
nerves on the rack. You could see strong men brace
themselves against it, set their teeth when they felt it
coming, and draw a long breath, when it was over,
as if they had just endured severe pain.

Many hours I watched the sea from the little round
window in my state room. It had a sort of fascination for me. It was a terribly beautiful sight. The

whole expanse one vast whirl, the mad waves leaping after each other and dashing against the ship, scattering sparkling phosphorescent bubbles all along as far as the eye could see. Sometimes, when the ship would give a deep lurch, the waves would run so high above the window that I was looking into the calm solid water, like clear ice, far below the raging foaming surface. At such times it was not difficult to imagine oneself in another world, and I don't think it would have surprised me much if a mermaid had peeped into the window.

Late on Tuesday evening there were signs that the worst fury of the storm was over, though there was but little difference in the appearance of the sea. I was watching eagerly for these favorable indications — but watching a long while without much faith in them. At last the change was too evident for doubt. Here and there a star glimmered out. It was reported that the sky was clearing up in the west. There was less to be heard of that horrid hissing noise which had pervaded the roar of the tempest. I shall never forget what welcome words those were, which an enthusiastic young friend called out to me as he passed my cabin at about midnight. "Good news!" cried he. "The barometer is going up steadily, and the captain has gone to bed!"

Good news indeed! The captain had never left the deck since Sunday evening — nearly sixty hours. The fact that he had now gone to bed was certainly a favorable omen. All sorts of alarming stories had been told among the passengers, because he had not been seen. He had been washed overboard, with several of the men! Two or three of the other officers were disabled! The ship was almost a wreck! Fortunately there was but little foundation for these alarming stories. No man had been lost, and none of the crew had been very seriously injured, except one poor fellow who had a hand badly crushed when the steering wheel was carried away. Two of his fingers were afterward amputated. The second officer had been dashed against the guards, with a force that bent an iron wire an inch in diameter, and was swept over the rail and flung upon the main deck, where he found himself with his head in a scupper-hole nearly a hundred feet from where he started. He was disabled for the rest of the voyage, except the last day, when he made his appearance with his arm in a sling. The captain escaped without any bruises, but his neck was all raw, when he was first seen after the storm, from the constant beating of the salt spray. Many blamed him severely for running the ship so near to destruction, but all were glad to see him again. He looked like a man who would fight to the death, with his short tight-curly sandy hair, his little sparkling eyes, red square face, glittering teeth, and thick bull neck. He was a model of strength and daring, and his ship was new, big and powerful — but how puny both had been in the contest with the elements!

On Wednesday morning there was a visible change for the better, though the sea was still running very high. The passengers were thankful and happy. Some venturesome ones made their way upon deck, to look at the damages done by the storm. The pilot-house was a complete wreck. The bowsprit had been carried away. All the topmasts were gone. Some of the life-boats were half-torn from their fastenings. Many other marks of its visitation had been left by the storm. Generally speaking, landsmen overrate the dangers of the situation when there is anything like rough weather at sea, and they have but little satisfaction in asking sailors what they thought about it, as the latter are apt to pooh-pooh their expressions of alarm. It is seldom that a sailor will admit that he has not seen worse storms. The case was different with this. The captain said that he had never been out in a more "nasty storm." He told the passengers that they might cross the Atlantic two hundred times and not encounter such another. The chief engineer, a man of great experience, said he had thought the ship was lost. She made one plunge which it seemed must be her last. The fifteen seconds of suspense following this thought were as long as fifteen minutes, he said. There was an old sea-captain among the passengers, who had commanded a packet ship between Liverpool and New York more than twenty years. He was my main stay. I had become quite intimate with him, and I know that during the storm he was as anxious as so cool a man could be. I had observed him watching the ship when she was laboring hardest. His fear was that she would break in two, under some of the fearful strains. But she was a grand ship, he said, and he could not sufficiently praise her. He, also, had never seen a storm that was at once so violent and so long.

Talk about these matters made the day pass quickly. Almost every body appeared to be rather glad, now that the danger was past, that we had undergone such an experience. It was something to talk about hereafter. Our escape was something we could be congratulated upon. It was something that none of us would ever forget. The remembrance of our great peril would add a zest to the fireside comforts of home. Mingled with all this talk there was a feeling of gratitude — earnest, too, I hope — to that Power who had held us in the hollow of his hand. We speculated much as to the progress the ship had made during the three days' storm. At noon the record was posted up. She had done but little more than one good day's work in the three. From Monday noon till Tuesday noon she made only thirty miles. Imagine what a desperate struggle that noble ship had gone through!

All this day (Wednesday) the sea was very rough. If it had not been so much more furious before, we should have thought the storm still a great one. It was on this day that an accident happened to the present writer, which he dislikes to tell, never having succeeded in eliciting the slightest sympathy from any hearer of his tale. On the contrary, generally he gets laughed at instead. But then, I know he would have told the story, had he seen the accident happen to any other unfortunate — so it shall be honestly set down here.

With infinite pains I had shaved and bathed and put on clean clothes. Not another man in the ship had risked the first-mentioned operation, either at his own hand or at the barber's. It was almost as bad as trying to shave on a tight rope, swaying back and forth, pitching hither and thither, according to the motion of the ship — but I persevered, and did the deed. Not a little proud was I when my remarkably clean appearance was noticed in the saloon, for by this time almost every man's beard was nearly a week old. Well, in an evil moment I accepted a challenge from a younger and more active man who dared me to run up with him to the upper deck, and examine the damages inflicted by the storm. He led the way, and got safely up the stairs. I followed—alas! that I did not lead! Just as my upper half appeared above the stairs, a big wave came over the stern of the ship, struck me in the middle, and wet down my lower half as thoroughly as though I had been dipped in the sea. It quite took my breath away, but I couldn't say any thing when I recovered it again. My thoughts were too deep for utterance. It was

12

less than half an hour since I had left my cabin, clean, smooth and smiling, when I returned, wet, dripping and miserable. My coat was a short one and was not wet, thanks at that moment to the judicious tailor who had persuaded me to adopt the style, in spite of my old-fashioned prejudices. My wet garments (why do I mention them?) were soon removed. I had but one dry pair left which were accessible. They were in a valise, which I as yet had had no occasion, or no ambition rather, to unlock. Where were my keys? I felt for them in all my pockets, but found them not. Horror upon horrors, they could not surely be lost! Yes, I was quite certain now, I had left them in Cork. I cannot describe the feeling of utter desolation which overwhelmed me when I at last gave up the search for the keys, and realized the full difficulties of my situation. I sat down on the sofa (how cold and scratchy its horse-hair cover was!) and gave myself up to despair. It was a tragical moment, and I felt ready to welcome another storm, be it ever so stormy. There hung those wet things, (which must not be mentioned) dripping aggravatingly, with at least a pail-full of nasty salt water absorbed in them. I could not go out to borrow a pair, for the hall was full of ladies, sitting on boxes, talking about the dangers we had passed through. My position was truly an embarrassing one. What did I care then for the trumpery dangers those women were magnifying so absurdly? How ridiculously short my coat was, and how I inwardly denounced the villian of a tailor who had enveigled me into the miserable skirtless thing, against my own better judgment! If there was a patient sufferer on that ship just then (I heard of one) it was not me. . . . . At last I was persuaded to search another set of pockets for the keys, and found them too where I had not the least notion they could be. How hastily I opened the valise, and how thankfully I put on those welcome things (which I am now almost tempted to mention), though they were quite too thin for ship wear, I must leave you to imagine, as I cannot describe my feelings. But I didn't trust the treacherous waves any more during the voyage, for I now had on my last pair.

If I had room I could tell about some queer talk I heard among the passengers, touching the storm and its dangers. What would have happened in such a case, and what we should have done if it had not been for such a thing. There were, in particular, certain speculations about the vessel — supposing it to be made in compartments, and one should get suddenly filled, whether the others would be equal to the emergency, and so on — which would amuse, I am sure, if they could be understood. But you know how people will talk on such an occasion. It is better that I should go on with the story of the voyage.

Thursday was a tolerably fair day, the first we had been favored with, then eight days out. Still the wind, what there was of it, was against us. By night the weather was thick again, and on Friday morning we were in another storm, only less severe than the last. It appeared to me that the ship rolled and plunged as frightfully as before. But I saw the danger was not so great. Yet it was excessively discouraging. Many who had kept up good courage entirely through the first storm, now lost all heart. I think there was more fear manifested now than ever before, for it seemed that the elements were bent upon our destruction. I noticed one young lady — a pretty willful little creature who had assumed the attentions of everybody as due to her by right — trying to play whist. She picked out her card, and minced and flirted, just as she had done the day before; but, suddenly, as the ship gave a deeper plunge than usual, and that horrible noise of the screw thrilled again through all nerves, she flung her cards upon the table, and covering her face in her hands, threw herself down on the seat, a picture of utter despair.

I observed many such indications. There was one gentleman the state of whose nerves was distressing to behold. He had been very much frightened all through the first storm and had the frankness to admit the fact. But he was not altogether hopeless then — now he gave up all for lost. I tried to divert his thoughts, and asked him to be my partner at a game of whist. He strove heroically for a while to give proper attention to the game, but every time that craunching noise was repeated, he would stop, lose the run of the game—his face blanched his chin quivering, and his eyes red with fear. At last he gave it up. He could not possibly, he said, control his nerves. "Something tells me," he added, "that something is going to happen to night." I think that no one felt anything but sympathy for his distress.

The storm continued nearly all night, but by morning had sensibly abated. Almost the first man I saw was the gentleman of whom I have spoken. He was queerly dressed. "Why, G——," said I, "what's the matter?" Then he poured out this story with great unction:

"You know," he began, "I told you last night that something told me something was going to happen. I went to my room at about one o'clock, but couldn't get to sleep. I told T——, who rooms with me, as I had told you, that something warned me something was going to happen that night. He laughed at me, told me the ship was going splendidly, that this was nothing compared with the other storm, and urged me to go to sleep. 'There's not a bit of danger,' said he; 'we're all right, I tell you!' The words were hardly out of his mouth when the door was dashed in, and I found myself on my back in the water, my hands in the air, feeling for something to grasp upon. I thought it was all over, and so did T——. Somebody called out, 'Stop the ship! stop the ship!' (T—— says it was me, but that's no matter.) Our cabin was full of water, and we were tossing about,

thinking the ship was going to pieces. We couldn't
get out till the old boatswain came to our help. You
know the old boatswain — weighs about two hundred
and fifty, with a face like the rising sun, and a voice
like a locomotive with a bad cold. 'What's the matter, boys?' says he. 'For God's sake, boatswain,'
said I, ' what kind of weather do you call this? Are
we all going to the bottom?' 'Oh, it's all right, sir,'
replied he, 'bootiful weather—bootiful weather, sir!'
—Wasn't that aggravating? And wasn't I right
last night? I knew something *was* going to happen,
for something told me so!"

I think he was quite jubilant over the fulfillment of
his prediction, though all his clothes were wet through
and he had been obliged to borrow one man's hat, another man's coat, and so on. His cabin was on the
upper deck, and it must have been a huge wave indeed which had overwhelmed it.

We encountered but little more bad weather on the
voyage. Saturday was not a very rough day. With
fair weather we should have been in New York that
morning — now we were more than a thousand miles
away. On Sunday, when the Morning Prayer was
read, the saloon was crowded, and I know that all
heartily joined in the Thanksgiving for our Deliver-
ance from the Storms. In the early part of the day
the weather was tolerably fair, but later it rained and
stormed a little, just enough to keep us all from being
too jubilant. Monday was a lovely day, and we felt

that we were in American waters. How happy all were when land birds flew into the rigging and we thought them like friends from home, come with good news to meet us on the way — how excited when the pilot came on board in the evening — how delighted the next morning when we saw the welcome land — how impatient to set foot on shore when we were detained about an hour at anchor — and how profoundly grateful to find ourselves once more upon the solid earth, the blessed Home land, — it is not given me to tell. The voyage was over — the dangers past — friends were waiting to welcome us — and we were "Home again!" Thank God.

XV.

CONSISTING MAINLY OF HINTS FOR TRAVELERS, WITH SOME
REFLECTIONS UPON THE TRIP, AND HERE AND THERE A
REMINISCENCE.

It is worth a man's while to go abroad if only to
realize the happiness of returning home again. I had
indulged in the pleasure of anticipation, in respect to
this, all the time I was away, and the result did not
disappoint me. No fact that I have written has been
set down with greater truth, or with more satisfaction
than this.

Another pleasure gained is that of retrospection.
The returned tourist has not been home long before
he begins to review the ground over which he has
passed. It is more than likely, that, as in my own
case, he will be asked so many questions about places
which he did not visit, as to make him think at first
that he has seen almost nothing. But the second
thought will dispel the illusion. It is hardly possible
but he must have brought away from Europe a thousand memories of places and things famous and beau-

tiful. The impressions on his mind may be cloudy and obscure, or they may be confused because there are so many of them; but a little dust brushed away, a little order in the arrangement, a little warming of the memory-plate before the fire of imagination, and soon the pictures become clear and distinct, and the tourist will make the journey, see the sights, and realize all his adventures over again. He will then be satisfied that instead of having seen almost nothing, he saw more than appeared to be possible until the retrospection placed the facts before him. A mere enumeration of the places he visited will be very likely to surprise him. From a glance at the record of my own brief summer holiday one may learn how much can be done in the way of traveling and sight-seeing in Europe in a very limited period. I was gone from home only four months. I was not a systematic traveler, by any means. Much more than I accomplished could be done in the same space of time by any tourist who would lay out his routes carefully and rigidly pursue them. Yet, in my careless, unmethodical fashion, I managed to spend one day in Bremen — nearly two weeks in Dresden, the capital of Saxony, witnessing the occupation of that city by the Prussians, the first important incident of the great campaign — a week in Berlin and Potsdam — five days at Cologne and "up the Rhine"—a few days at Wiesbaden, Frankfort and Homburg — two days at Heidelberg and one at Strasburg — ten days in Switzerland,

12*

stopping at Basle, Berne, Interlaken and the Lakes, and at the Swiss metropolis, Geneva—more than two weeks in Paris, including Versailles and Fontaine-bleau—nearly a whole month in London—about ten days more in England, making visits to Portsmouth, the Isle of Wight, Leamington, Stratford, Warwick, Kenilworth, Chester and Liverpool—concluding with a week in Ireland, during which I visited Dublin, Bray and the County Wicklow, the Lakes of Killarney, Cork and Queenstown, not forgetting Blarney, its Castle, its Groves, and its Blarney Stone. A pretty good summer's trip, certainly.

The tourist realizes one of the greatest advantages gained in foreign travel after he has returned home. He will be surprised at the greatly enhanced interest discovered in much of his reading. It was but the other day that I read a little story, the scene of which was laid in Switzerland. There was not much of the tale itself,—in fact I should not have read it at all except that in glancing over it my eye caught some familiar names — but the incidents occurred in places where I had traveled, the lovers climbed mountains together that I had seen, the *denouement* took place at a hotel where I had sojourned — and there were all my experiences in that charming country brought before my imagination as vividly as if they were events of only yesterday! Some pleasure of this sort occurs almost every day. The ponderous "leaders" of the London *Times* are not imaginative reading, generally speaking. I have not, unfortunately, (or otherwise !) many spare minutes for that kind of literature. Yet, not long ago, I read one of the Thunderer's articles with wonderful interest, and my imagination was more excited therein than it usually is by the most thrilling pages of poetry or romance. The article was upon the withdrawal of the British diplomatic representative from the Court of Saxony. In other days the subject would have possessed no interest for me, but now every sentence was full of matter that brought up recollections of Dresden, and my brief stay there, and my hurried departure therefrom. How many reminiscences grew out of this single paragraph ! —

"The name of Saxony, its dynasty, its territorial demarcation, are suffered to remain; but foreign diplomacy knows it no more. Some of the stateliest mansions of Dresden are left untenanted; the shine is taken off its Court dresses; some of the brightest stars fade from the galaxy of the Opera. The club, the terrace, the gardens miss some of their most distinguished loungers. Dresden's great attractions are there still; the unmatched Picture Gallery; the unique Holbein; the loveliest Raphael: but, alas! who cares for the *entrée* to a mediatized Court? for balls and receptions for which no Legation any longer gives cards?"

I saw it all before me again — the great event that had presaged this change! I saw again that melancholy march of the poor old King with his little army out of the beautiful city, and the triumphant entry of the powerful Prussians. I lounged again through the

Great Gallery and had bright visions of those glorious pictures.   All the attractions of the German Flor-
ence were spread before me again, and I realized
again the meaning of the German friend, who, in describing Dresden to me before I left home, had
summed it up in this brief exclamation: "Dresden?
Paradise!" *

Friends ask me if it is worth while to go to Europe
for a single summer.   Most surely it is.   Take a year,
if you can—but if you can't spare more than a sum-

---

* As I gave the King of Saxony's Proclamation on leaving Saxony (see
page 28) it occurs to me that it will be proper to give his address to his
people on returning.   Here it is:

"SAXONS!—

"After a long and grievous separation, after a season teeming with
"great events, I return once more among you.

"I know what you have suffered and borne, and I have sympathized
"with my whole heart, but I know also with what firm fidelity you have
"adhered through all trials to your native Prince.   This thought has been,
"next to my trust in God, my best consolation in the hours of sadness with
"which by the inscrutable decrees of Providence, both you and I have
"been afflicted.   It gives me new courage to resume my old daily task.

"With all my former affection increased, if it be possible, by the num-
"erous evidences of attachment which I have received, I shall devote the
"days which it may please God to grant me to healing the wounds of the
"country, to advancing its prosperity, to maintaining law and justice, and
"to the judicious development of our political institutions.   In the per-
"formance of that great task I rely upon the support of the representa-
"tives of the country, before whom I shall go with the frankness and
"confidence of past times.

"With the fidelity with which I supported the old Confederation I shall
"adhere to the new union into which I now enter, and I shall do all that
"lies in my power to render it as fruitful as possible for our limited coun-
"try and for our great common Fatherland.

"May the Almighty bless our common efforts, and may Saxony remain
"as she was before — a country of peace, order, of intellectual culture and
"morality, and in the fear of God!

        "TOPLITZ, Oct. 26.   JOHN."

mer, take that. Of course it is better to do what you
can do thoroughly, than to merely race over the
ground and be only able to say that you have visited
such and such places. But if you cannot see all the
note-worthy objects of any place, to see half of them
is better than to see none at all. I know that many
think it hardly desirable to go to any interesting
place unless sufficient time can be given to do justice
to its attractions. But I think differently. "Make
the most of your opportunities" is as good a maxim
to guide the tourist in his travels as in any of the
more practical occupations of life. It is the habit of
Europeans to laugh at the rapid pace which Americans keep up in their pleasure traveling. "How is it,"
said a gentleman to me in London, "that you manage
to get over so much ground in a single summer? We
go to Scotland, or Germany, or to the sea-side, or
somewhere else, for a month or two, and that's all we
think of doing in one summer. But you Americans
go all over Europe in three or four months, and call
it pleasure! We should call it hard work." I reminded him that Americans had to travel three or
four thousand miles before they reached Europe, and
as many more to return. If the time was sufficient
the pecuniary consideration would prevent most of
them from coming every summer. Having journeyed
so far before reaching the starting point with Europeans, and not expecting to make such a trip very
soon again, they are not satisfied with a visit to any

one country, but must see all they can in the time afforded them.   It is all very well for people who can go one summer to one place and another to another to take their time at each, but unless Americans spend their holidays at home they cannot do their pleasure-traveling in that leisurely way.   My friend was good enough to say he had not looked at the matter in that light before, and that there was some method in our madness after all.

I have spoken of "the pecuniary consideration." It must not be inferred that the expense of a summer spent in Europe needs to be very much greater than the same length of time spent at Saratoga or any other fashionable home watering-place.   True, traveling and personal expenses are apt to be considerably larger than some popular Guide-Books estimate; but unless the tourist is heedlessly extravagant six or seven dollars a day make an abundant provision for hotel bills and railway fare.   This, of course, does not include purchases.   For "shopping" no rules can be laid down.   But, whatever the expense may be, I have yet to meet the returned tourist who regrets either the time or the money he had spent on such a holiday.

Shopping in foreign cities: it is of two sorts — to shop for one's self, and to shop for one's friends at home. In regard to the former, if I were not painfully conscious of how utterly useless it would be, judging from my own experience, I should advise all tourists to eschew that seductive occupation as much as possible; but, in regard to the latter, I have no scruple at all — my emphatic advice is, like that offered by Mr. Punch, "To persons about to marry:—*Don't!*" To oblige a friend is one of the pleasantest things in life, and nobody, I trust, can accuse this writer of failing to reap that pleasure, both in season and out of season—and sometimes beyond all reason, too. I was not churlish about executing such commissions abroad as certain friends requested of me; and I am happy in the thought that those friends were not only satisfied but gratified at what I did in that way for them. But notwithstanding all this, I must candidly say, in reference to making purchases for others, that the anxiety which the tourist will feel, lest the articles should be injured or lost, or should not prove satisfactory, is hardly compensated by the pleasure he will experience in having obliged a friend, even supposing the result does convince him that all his fears had been for naught.

Something too much of this, however. It is more agreeable to speak about shopping for one's self. To the American in foreign cities the inducements to spend money are almost irresistible. The temptations of good St. Anthony were nothing in comparison. He sees so many beautiful things that are not to be seen at all in his own country—or that *he* never saw, at any rate—and the prices appear so reasonable, in many cases, compared with his ideas of their value, that the chances are fearfully against the American's prudence, and he is likely to buy, not only a great many things which he may perhaps want, but an almost equal number of things, also, which he does not want.

I remember a case in point — in fact am not likely to forget it as long as time shall last with me. The person of whom I speak (I hate to be too personal in these cases) wanted to buy a clock — a nice clock, of course. He was directed to one of the largest manufactories in the world, and a most bewildering array in the immense show rooms was displayed for his examination. More clocks than he could count, and all handsome, for it was a concern that made only the finer kinds. Neat clocks, beautiful clocks, rich clocks, classic clocks, gorgeous clocks! Clocks encased in marble of all colors, in bronze, in gilt, in crystal, with devices the most artistic. It was difficult to select from so many, but he did, after much comparison one with another, decide upon one which was suitable in every way; not too handsome to look out of place when it should be at home, and not too expensive either. Here he should have rested his case, settled, and left the premises. But the polite attendant insisted upon his inspecting the stock further — especially some unfinished works designed for the Great Exposition. At last his attention was directed to a clock of a peculiarly graceful device, with vases to match. He admired the set much — so much, indeed, that he was deaf to the whispers of prudence, and bought the rather expensive things instead of the more modest article he had at first chosen.

It had been well enough, perhaps, if the matter had ended here; but the worst is yet to be told. This foolish person realized his folly, after having slept upon it, and repented. Next day he returned to the scene of his temptation, fully resolved to reverse his last decision (as the money had not been paid yet) and go back to his first choice. Another look at that clock satisfied him that it was just what he wanted. The polite attendant was as polite as before, and quite content to let the fickle purchaser have his way. "But will not Monsieur once again look at the other, so elegant?" Monsieur did look once again, and that look was so long that he once again changed his mind and determined to keep the clock, so elegant. But, mark the sequel! On his way out he passed the other again — the "sensible clock" as he called it — and bought that too!

Attempting subsequently to explain this curious result of a prudential afterthought, the foolish person said it was a Compromise — the only basis upon which any great and intricate question, where two opposing principles are involved, ever could be settled. He bought the elegant clock as a concession to his taste, and his admiration for the beautiful and the progressive; and then took the sensible one as a concession to the conservative and prudent side of his character!

This story about two clocks, I think, may fitly close my disquisition upon "Shopping," as it affords a doubly striking example of one danger against which I would warn fellow-travelers.

But to return to the matter of traveling expenses in Europe. If a party of four or five persons travel together the expense to each will be lessened, and the pleasure increased, provided there is a fair degree of congeniality between them. The admission fee to many places is the same for a single visitor as for a party. Carriage hire is a considerable item in the tourists' expenses, and that, of course, will be reduced by such a combination. But the advantages gained by traveling in a party are more apparent at hotels than anywhere else. It is pleasant to have friendly company at your meals, whether you take them at the public table, or in private rooms as is generally the case in Europe. If you happen to be in a country whose customs and language are unfamiliar, you do not feel half so much annoyance at your own blunders if you can only have the blunders of friends to laugh at as well. You can bear one another out, as it were, if several are in the same boat.

But very little trouble, however, is experienced for want of the native language in any part of Europe, so far as my observation goes. And I heard this view corroborated by most of the friends I met abroad. This is particularly true of Paris, where you can scarcely find a shop or hotel at which English is not

spoken. I have known people who found this preva-
lence of the English tongue an objection to Paris.

"What shall I do in Paris," said I to a lady I met
in Switzerland, "without a word of French at my
command?"

"Oh, you will have no trouble on that score," she
replied; you will find the people only too ready to
speak English. I found it too provoking, sometimes,
when in a shop speaking my best French and getting
along nicely, as I thought, with the shopman. Just as
sure as I spoke in English to the friend who was with
me, the shopman would address me immediately in as
good English as my own, and give me no chance to
practice my French after that! They would not let
you speak French if you could!"

For satisfactory reasons I never tried it on, to be
sure, but I have no doubt that the lady's illustration
of the difficulty was a correct one.

One thing that astonishes the American in Europe is the number of his countryman that he continually comes in contact with, no matter where he goes.
I know of no greater pleasure abroad than that of
meeting friends from home; and, in fact, many people
are inclined in a foreign land to regard all fellow-coun-
trymen as friends. Sometimes this friendliness is
pleasant — sometimes not. Of course, in countries
where politeness is more the rule than with us, it be-
hooves Americans to accept advances from their com-
patriots graciously; but a certain degree of caution

is frequently wholesome and necessary. An instance of this occurred with me in Paris. I had just left the office of Messrs. Munroe & Co., the great American bankers, when a man whom I had noticed with a not very favorable impression, followed, overtook and stopped me.

"I beg your pardon, Sir," he said, "but might I ask what part of the States you came from?"

"You may, Sir," I replied.

And he did — and then I told him. Whereupon it immediately occurred to him that he knew Buffalo very well indeed.

"In fact," he said, "I was there in '36."

"I was not," I told him.

After a good deal of beating about the bush — but not until my constitutional impatience was beginning to get the better of my native politeness — he made his object known.

"The truth is, Sir," he said, "I am in a very unpleasant predicament. I am in need of money to-day, and have been expecting a remittance some time. It will surely come to-morrow, and the favor I would beg — —"

"But I fear you will think it strange," he added, parenthetically.

"Not at all," I assured him; "it does not surprise me in the least."

"Well, Sir," he continued, "I wish to borrow a trifling sum until to-morrow. *Could* you oblige me?

I will meet you in Munroe's office to-morrow — when I shall receive my remittance — and discharge the obligation."

"*Un*-fortunately," said I, with a mental reservation of the emphasized syllable, "I leave Paris early to-morrow morning, and it will be impossible for me, therefore, to accommodate you."

"But," I went on to say, as he was about to vary the proposition, "undoubtedly Messrs. Munroe & Co., or our Minister, Mr. Bigelow, would be only too happy to serve you, if you will state your case to them as convincingly as you have to me."

He evidently saw it was useless to press the matter any further, and so we parted, with much mutual politeness; he, evincing no trace of suspicion that I distrusted him — I, satisfied that his feelings were not wounded if he was honest, and that I was no victim of misplaced confidence if he was not.

There are many other topics that might be treated at considerable length, in this my closing epistle — topics interesting chiefly to those who purpose going abroad. I made it a rule, however, in writing my letters to mention briefly at the time such facts of this sort as struck me most forcibly; thus scattering through them (though all too rarely, I fear — like plums in a poor man's pudding) certain hints and suggestions not altogether without value, I would fain hope, to such chance readers of that class as those letters had, or as this book may find. To take up these slightly-touched topics again, though the excuse that I have now more room to do them justice might be an allowable excuse perhaps, would be only to make short stories long, whereas it is a much more popular plan to make long stories short; and I am thus debarred from speaking about several matters that I have been questioned upon, since my return.

But the gracious reader does not, I am sure, expect me to attempt a competition with any Hand-Book in giving directions to travelers, and I can therefore rest satisfied that sins of omission will be the lightest offences discovered in these pages. I cheerfully recommend people who are expecting to make a foreign trip, to get all the Hand-Books they can obtain — "Harper's," "Murray's," "Bædeker's," and others — and to get them early, and read them too. It is hardly possible but some information will be derived from the poorest of them, worth more than the cost of the book, and the traveler will soon regard his "Guide" as a companion and friend as well.

My task may be ended in a single closing observation: Apart from the new pleasures which the tourist will realize after he arrives home, as well as abroad (for surely my own experience is common with that of all other travelers), it appears to me that a tour in Europe, be it ever so brief, cannot fail to be useful to Americans. They must return home with more enlightened views of men and things, and a more rational and catholic love of their own country and its institutions with less prejudice against other countries and people. The beautiful Old World will have excited their admiration without diminishing their patriotic love for the New. After such an absence, also, it seems to me, a man must come home with friendships strengthened and renewed, and enmities forgotten or forgiven.

THE END.

www.ingramcontent.com/pod-product-compliance
Lightning Source LLC
Chambersburg PA
CBHW060616030726
47498CB00005B/1697